THE SCORECARD

MAREN MOORE

Copyright © 2022 by Maren Moore/R. Holmes
All rights reserved.
No part of this book may be reproduced in any form or by any electronic or mechanical means, including information storage and retrieval systems, without written permission from the authors, except for the use of brief quotations in a book review.
This is a work of fiction. Names, characters, places, businesses, companies, organizations, locales, events and incidents either are the product of the authors' imagination or used fictitiously. Any resemblances to actual persons, living or dead, is unintentional and co-incidental. The authors do not have any control over and do not assume any responsibility for authors' or third-party websites or their content.

Cover Design: Cat with TRC DESIGNS
Formatting: Maren Moore

For Kayla,
Because without you, this book would have never happened. I love you always.

And Jack Harlow. Because.. obviously.

PLAYLIST

Steady Heart- Kameron Marlowe
chaotic- Tate McRae
As It Was- Harry Styles
Never Till Now- Ashley Cooke
makeup sex- Machine Gun Kelly, blackbear
Fingers Crossed- Lauren Spencer- Smith
From Austin- Zach Bryan
When You're Gone- Shawn Mendes
Look at the Mess I'm In- Danielle Bradbery
Holy Water- Brett Eldredge
Angels- Thomas Rhett
Leave You Alone- Kane Brown

To listen to the full playlist click here.

ACKNOWLEDGMENTS

As always, my favorite part of every book I write, is the part where I tell the world about the people who make my dreams possible.

There are so many people that work behind the scenes, and this book is a special one. Not only because Graham is everyones favorite character, but because I struggled for almost four months with the worst writers block I've ever had.

It was impossible to write. I cried, I got angry, I mediated, I read, I didn't touch or even look at my computer for weeks. It took so much to finally get to the point where the words were here again.

So, thank you to everyone who believed in me and gave me words of encouragement during this time.

Without you, this book would not have happened. I owe it all to you.

Thank you to my amazing team for standing by me and encouraging me, supporting me, and keeping things running. Katie, Amanda, Christina… without you three, I would be a hot mess. period. I love you girls so much and am so thankful for my dream team.

Holly Renee. Words will never be enough to tell you how much I love you. You have no clue how precious you are to me. My twin flame.

Kayla, I already dedicated this book to you, but here's another spot to tell you how much I love you and how thankful I am for your friendship. Besties forever.

Mia, I love you. Always. Your guidance, and friendship is everything to me.

Haley, Siobhan, and Bri... my beta babes. Thank you so much for your input, and help making my books what they are. I owe it all to y'all.

Ellie, Kerry, Sahara, & Jaz— my hype girls! Love you girls so much.

My Puck bunnies & my street/arc team— Thank you for being so supportive and my favorite place on the internet. Without you, my world wouldn't turn.

And to every reader who has taken a chance on me. Whether you loved or hated my work, thank you for picking it up and taking a chance.

EMERY

ONE

I'M *OFFICIALLY* LICENSED to practice law in the state of Illinois.

I fucking did it, and it feels incredible to say it.

Emery Davidson, Attorney-at-law.

I passed the bar exam, after studying for what felt like forever, and of course manifesting the hell out of that shit. Mindset is everything after all.

And what better way to celebrate graduating law school and passing the bar exam on your first try, than getting drunk on Dom Perignon in your older brother's stupidly large mansion with some of your girls?

I honestly can't think of anything better, but then again, I really can't think clearly *at all* right now. Not after who knows how many glasses of expensive champagne, courtesy of the same hotshot NHL brother, that I've had tonight. After spending the last seven years with my head buried in books, and practically never resurfacing for air, I'm so excited to be able to breathe easier and know that it's over.

"You did it, bitch!" Lea, my work bestie and lifeline for the past two years, squeals, holding up her glass. "Not that I had any doubt. We all know when Emery Davidson sets her mind on something, it is happening, come hell or high water."

My friends laugh in unison because well... she's right.

Tenacious, driven, and ambitious.

Those are just a few of the traits that describe my personality, and some of the best, I might add, which is why they're listed on my Tinder profile that I made after a bottle of wine and never touched again last week.

Lea and Ana are my girls: two of the closest people to me and the only *real* friends I made at the University of Chicago through my law school journey. I seriously wouldn't have made it without them. They were there through the sleepless nights. The long, endless nights where my eyes blurred after reading over countless law textbooks until I passed out on my books. Nights where I was so exhausted, I couldn't hold my head up any longer. Through breakups and all of our girls' nights out at The Lush Library, the bar down the street from the law library.

All that's missing tonight is Holland, my best friend since middle school and now my *actual* sister for life after she and Reed, my brother, started dating and then tied the knot a few years ago.

They're currently in Disney World with Evan, my nephew, and I miss the shit out of them.

Buuuuut... I am thankful that Reed and Holland left me to house-sit for the week in a house big enough for its own episode on *MTV Cribs*. Not to mention, they left the key to the liquor cabinet and I've been a struggling student for the past seven years, okay? My brother plays for the NHL; he can afford to give up a few bottles of Dom to celebrate something as momentous as his baby sister passing the bar exam.

Taking the bottle from Ana, I grip the neck and spin

around in a circle, holding it above my head as my hips sway to Jack Harlow on the surround sound.

"I'm just so glad to be done. I'm not picking up another textbook for at least a year." I laugh, bringing the bottle to my lips for a long swig. The bubbles are smooth, rich, and luxurious. My favorite way to celebrate. "I just feel so ... *free*. I'm twenty-seven and single, on the way to becoming a partner in my law firm. Well, that's the dream at least."

Lea's sing-song laugh echoes off the marble walls. "And girl, it's sickening how you have such a great ass with all the Starbucks and cheap beer we've lived off through law school. Seriously."

I smirk.

I do have a great ass, but that's because even though I've spent more time studying than sleeping in the last few years, I always have time for squats. It's one of the very few "rules" I set for myself fresh into college. Squats come first, top-shelf tequila second and steering clear of commitment third. At least where men are included. Outside of those rules? Anything goes.

That's why I picked Landon; he was... fun. A tall, intelligent, averagely handsome paralegal at the law firm I work for. He was also perfectly fine with being the 'hookup-only' guy. Except he turned out to be a douche and cared more about his status at the firm than he did me.

Not that I'm heartbroken over our "breakup." If anything, it was casual, neither of us really giving enough of the other to be invested, but he did break up with me over a two-sentence text.

So that sucked. But, whatever.

As always, I bounced back.

Like the bad bitch I am.

"This Dom is some serious shit, I am dddddrunk." Lea

drags out the word, mumbling into her glass. Her curtain of black hair falls forward, and a drunken smirk sits on her lips.

"Same," I agree, nodding my head.

Her black hair glistens under the chandelier as she whips her head around and grins wickedly. "You know, it was so nice of Reed to let you stay here while they were gone."

I nod. That's Reed, he's the best guy I know. My best friend, but also the most annoying man on the planet, but I think that's a brother thing.

"I know, it's been nice. My house pales in comparison to this place." I gesture at the living room. Holland and Reed spent months going over plans, and tweaking everything to make their forever home perfect, and it shows. It's beautifully thought-out and it fits their family perfectly.

"You're probably so used to it by now, but it is so insane to me that your brother plays in the NHL. Like, holy shit. He's a *celebrity*."

I shrug, tossing my hair over my shoulder. "He's been playing hockey for years, so it's second nature, I guess. It was kind of an adjustment at first. People recognizing him whenever we went out in public, throwing their underwear on his lawn, that sort of thing. Now it's just who he is. His job is hockey, but when he's at home, he's just Reed."

"No offense, but I'd throw my underwear at your brother, Em." Ana giggles. "Actually, I have a *serious* crush on Hudson. He's just... ugh, I would do anything for one night with him. Give me one night and it's over for all the rest of those puck bunnies."

My nose crinkles in distaste. I mean Hudson is an attractive guy, but one... he's an athlete.

Number one on my "fuck no list." And two... he's *Hudson*. He's one of my brother's best friends, which immediately puts him at the bottom of my "would you rather" list. Well, that and that night is seared into my memory. The night I found out exactly who Graham was.

I've grown up around athletes, specifically hockey players, and while there are lots of them I love, you couldn't pay me to date one. I know exactly what goes on in those locker rooms. It's bad enough that I have to hear my brother's friends talk about puck bunnies twenty-four-seven.

No thanks.

I'll stick to my business casual men who leave before the night is over.

Casual is the only type of commitment I'm interested in, period. Once upon a time, I gave my heart to someone who didn't deserve it. An athlete who was more worried about fame and sticking his dick into girls that weren't me. Now, I know better. My mom always said if it isn't a lesson, then it's a blessing. And I consider it a blessing that the truth was revealed before I did something crazy like marry him.

Honesty means everything to me. And knowing what most hockey players are like?

Not for me. Never again.

"Uh huh, nope," Lea says, shaking her head. "It's all Graham Adams for me. I don't even care that he's a manwhore. Those dimples, they melt me. And talk about beautiful. That man was built by God himself just for women's enjoyment. Seriously, dirty blonde hair, dipped in honey eyes? I can't. Not to mention he's like six foot four. Tall guys are hot. Do not even get me started on what he looks like shirtless. I saw him jogging on some gossip site and I almost dropped my cold brew."

My eyes roll, and I gag instinctively. "Eww."

Out of all of my brother's friends, Graham is dead last on my list. And do you want to know why?

Because his ego is the size of the arena he plays in. Not to mention, he's the biggest playboy in the entire NHL and I know that for a fact. Why you ask? Because of *that* night.

My mind drifts back to the night I knew that I wanted absolutely *nothing* to do with Graham Adams...

My hands tighten around the handle of the hockey stick I'm clutching for dear life.

Of course, the night I'm being the dutiful sister and house-sitting for Reed and Holland, someone is trying to break in.

Thump.

This time I hear the commotion outside accompanied with what sounds like a... groan?

What the hell?

If this is a burglar, they're absolutely shit at it.

I hold the stick higher as the door handle jiggles, swallowing down the fear in my throat.

God, what if they like... shoot me or something?

I barely have time to process the thought because the door swings open, and two figures, blanketed in the shadow of the dark, come tumbling through the front door and I take off full speed toward them, hockey stick raised high over my head.

Honestly, the battle cry that leaves my lips in the process of all of this is pretty fucking impressive, if I say so myself.

I bring the stick down on one of their heads and hear a loud, deep groan.

"What the fuck, Emery?"

Wait, how do they know my name? Oh God, maybe Reed has a psycho stalker.

Raising the hockey stick again, I'm about to smash it down on the psycho's head once more when the figure next to him starts laughing.

Manically.

Actually...

Is he giggling?

"Emery, it's Graham and Briggs. Can you please put down the weapon? Jesus."

Seconds later, the foyer light flicks on, illuminating the culprits.

Graham Adams and Briggs Wilson.

My brother's idiot best friends and teammates on his hockey team, the Avalanches.

"Are you serious?" I mutter, lowering the stick but only slightly. "It's almost midnight. Why in the hell are you two stumbling into my brother's house? I thought you were thieves!"

Graham smiles, revealing two dimples on his cheeks. "Well, we had a little bit too much to drink and Reed told us to crash here. Should've warned ya. Sorry babe."

Too good looking for his own good, Briggs snickers next to him, "Sup Em."

His eyes travel down the length of my body and in the... commotion, I forgot to pull on a sweatshirt. I'm clad in only one of Reed's old t-shirts that falls barely mid-thigh.

I bring the stick down and lean it back against the front door in its rightful place, then cross my arms. "I should make you both sleep outside after scaring me like that."

Briggs apologizes, but Graham stumbles slightly toward the kitchen. "I'm fucking starving. I know Reed's got the hookup on food, so I'm gonna eat real quick before we crash."

Briggs nods. "Fuck yes, let's go."

My feet stay rooted in place, and I just shake my head. I love my brother, dearly. I do.

But he and his friends aren't the smartest bunch.

"Clean up whatever you take out," I call behind them.

"You got it, babe!"

Babe.

Annoying.

I pad back to the couch, and press play on Law and Order before taking my spot again. Thirty minutes pass, and I can't focus with how loud Dumb and Dumber are being in there, so I press pause once more and walk toward the kitchen.

Before I walk in, I overhear Graham and Briggs talking. I press myself against the wall of the hallway and peer around the doorframe.

"Dude, Emery is hot as fuck. I just need one night with her," Briggs says, biting his fist.

Graham shakes his head, a shudder racking his wide shoulders, then pauses. A second passes before he speaks, "Gross. That would be like fucking Reed, and while the dude is extraordinarily handsome... fuck no."

Briggs laughs, tossing another chip in his mouth. "You're telling me you wouldn't give her the D?"

"Absolutely fucking not. Look, even if she wasn't Reed's sister, I still wouldn't be interested. She's not my type and I'm pretty sure she wouldn't be yours either."

"Yeah? Why not?"

Shrugging, Graham takes a bite out of the leftover pizza that was in the fridge. "She's too sassy. She's on the "I'm too independent for anyone, men suck, yada-yada. I like my women a little more... agreeable. Plus, she's not that hot."

Fucking asshole. Egotistical dick licker.

I own that shit. I am who I am, and I'm not changing for anyone, and especially not a man. I'm confident and independent, and I don't rely on a man to prove it. I'm way too hot to be listening to this crap spewing from Graham Adam's mouth.

Not that I would let him touch me anyway, but his words still sting. Rejection hangs in the air. Before tonight, I thought

Graham was maybe... cute, like a puppy that isn't the brightest bulb in the box. An idiot, sure. But this...? I was completely wrong. I guess there's a first time for everything.

Briggs shoves him lightly. "Shut the fuck up, you're drunk."

Graham nods. "Shitfaced. I'm headed to bed." He pops the remainder of the pizza into his mouth and drains the water bottle in front of him. "See you in the morning. Don't forget, we've got that appearance at the arena. Still trying to fix your reputation, dick."

I push off from the hallway wall and dart back to the living room, seething the entire way.

What a fucking dick.

The next morning, I wake up with Graham standing over me. Popping one eye open, I peer up and see the smug grin on his lips. His dark blonde hair is tousled, like he just woke up, and he's still wearing last night's clothes.

"Why are you creepily hovering over me?"

He smirks and holds out a coffee cup from Starbucks. "Got you coffee. As a sorry for stumbling in so late last night. We went out with some guys from the team, and they brought out shots," His shoulders shake as he shudders. "Never drinking tequila again."

I think back to the conversation I overheard last night, and anger bubbles inside me again.

"No thanks."

Sitting up, I stretch and get up, sashaying toward the kitchen in search of a Nespresso pod.

I wouldn't touch that coffee if it was the last cup on the planet.

"Uh why?" he says, trailing behind me.

I whip around to face him. "Is there a reason you're still here?"

"Because I brought you coffee."

Kind of funny that to my face he's flirty and charming as can be but last night was a completely different story when he thought no one was listening. Clearly, he's the kind of man who can't be trusted.

"Mmm. Sorry, but I'm way too independent to take coffee from a man."

His mouth opens, then closes, and before he can speak, Briggs strolls through the door. He's got a red spot on his cheek and dried drool along the corner of his mouth.

"Run along boys."

"Thanks for letting us crash, Em," Briggs calls from over his shoulder. "Let's go Romeo," he says to Graham.

Graham stares at me for another beat, then shakes his head and follows behind Briggs.

I shouldn't let his rejection affect me, seeing as how I didn't want it in the first place, but now more than ever, I know exactly why I don't do athletes.

They're all the same.

Probably great guys, but when it comes to relationships? There's no one worse.

Guys like Graham Adams will never have the chance to break my heart.

"Earth to Em." Lea snaps her fingers in my face, bringing me back to the present. "You totally zoned out, where'd you go?"

"Just thinking. You know, I'm kinda shocked that you'd pick Graham. I totally thought you'd go for Asher. Hot and nerdy, with a dash of muscle. Totally your type," I tease Lea.

Wait, that gives me an idea.

"Oh my god, I just had the best idea. Be right back." I dash into the kitchen, straight to Reed's "junk drawer" that looks like

Marie Condo herself organized it and pull out a piece of paper and a pen, then rejoin the girls back in the living room.

When I walk through the door, I hold the paper up. "Since we're picking our favorites. How about we rate them? The top ten players on the Avalanche team that if we were forced to spend a night with, we would spend one hot night with. PILF. Player I'd like to fuck. A scorecard of sorts."

Lea's eyes widen, but Ana grins wickedly, "Let's do it."

"C'mon Lea. It's just for fun. You know I'd rather burn every article of Lululemon in my closet than touch a hockey player. I promise I'll toss it before Reed gets home," I tell her.

Sitting down between them, I number the paper from one to ten.

"So, who are we putting first? And please don't say Adams or I'm going to vomit all over this couch." I grimace.

Ana takes another sip of her champagne as she considers her picks. Surprisingly, it's Lea that speaks first. "Definitely Asher. I think he's a solid choice. Loyal, super-hot, stays out of the headlines,"

I nod. "You're right. He's the safe choice. But are we rating them on who we'd settle down with or who we'd want to have the hottest, sweatiest sex with?"

Lea's cheeks heat, and she groans. "You're right. Your brother's gotta go first."

"I cannot put my brother's name on a scorecard of players I'd like to fuck, Lea. Gross. Maybe he can have an honorable mention or something."

Ana laughs. "Yeah, my vote's Hudson."

"What about Matthews? He's hot, and he has a great ass."

"Yes!" We all say together, and I scribble his name in my messy handwriting on the top spot. We spend the next few minutes tossing names onto the list in ranking order.

"Listen Em, I know you have a strong distaste for him... but Graham's gotta be number five. Honestly, he's probably number one, but for you, we've moved him down."

I groan. "He's an egotistical douche."

Ana nods. "But he's a hot douche, and who cares if he's a douche if he's got a big dick and makes you have vaginal orgasms?"

We've all heard the "locker-room" talk that made it out of the locker room, especially about Adams and his puck bunnies. I'm definitely anti-Graham, but objectively speaking, I guess he's a tad bit attractive.

Annnnd, I'm outvoted.

"Fine. Adams, number five." I begrudgingly write his name on the list, and we move on until we have all ten spots filled in.

Briggs
Hudson
Asher
Matthew
Graham

A solid list, if I do say so myself, even though, in actuality, I wouldn't touch any of these men with a ten-foot pole, but it's still fun to see where they rank when compared together.

"What's your deal with the no-athlete thing anyway, Em?" Ana asks. "You're like surrounded by hot hockey players."

I shrug. "I had a thing, a long time ago, with a hockey guy, and you know I don't repeat the same mistakes twice. He was a cheating asshole who made a complete fool of me. No one really even knew we were seeing each other. I kept it a secret because I didn't want to deal with Reed grilling me and giving me the third degree, then going all psycho big brother on him. I don't know, most hockey players are players and unable to commit to anything, unless it's a puck bunny for the night. So, no athletes for me. Not just hockey players. Plus, I've been around them my entire life. While I love them, I would never date one. I know exactly how they are."

Lea's eyes soften, and she reaches out to rub my arm sympathetically. "Guys are dicks. I'm just glad that you and Landon are done. He was a dickhole."

I suck in a breath, nodding. "He *was* fairly... dull." My eyes drift down to the scorecard in my hand, pausing over Graham's name again.

There was a time, back when he was first drafted to the Avalanches, that I thought he was cute, and I don't know, before I learned that he's the biggest manwhore on the team and doesn't care about anything but his ego, I might have said yeah had he asked me out, despite my no-athlete rule, maybe I might have even broken my rules for him.

Now that I know who he really is? *Never.*

The guy has a different girl on speed dial for Monday through Sunday. Seriously? Who does that? He probably doesn't even remember their names, just calls them by the day of the week that he sleeps with them.

Reed let that slip at family dinner last year, and after that night when Graham stumbled into Reed's house, I've never looked at him the same.

Like, don't get me wrong, I'm all about having fun and hooking up. Serious relationships are not and never will be my thing. I like the freedom, but I don't treat anyone as if they're disposable because that's not who I am, and I definitely would never shit-talk someone in their brother's kitchen, knowing they were in the other room.

"Anyway, athletes just are not my thing. I'm casually

dating, not tying myself down to anyone or anything and enjoying being the 'cool aunt.' I'm perfectly fine being the single girl."

Lea and Ana nod in agreement.

Why waste my youthful years? No thanks.

"Okay girls, as fun as that was, I'm starving, and I need tacos. Let's go." I grin, unfolding my crossed legs from the couch and skipping toward the kitchen. I set the scorecard on the counter by the pantry and get to work, making us my mama's famous street tacos.

By the time we've finished our tacos, the bottles of Dom are gone, and it's well after three a.m. We've laughed until our stomachs hurt so to end the night, we settle on the couch and put on reruns of *One Tree Hill*.

I make a mental note to clean everything up in the morning since my eyes are heavy, and my limbs are loose from the champagne. Reed has the comfiest couch in the world, which means I drift off ten minutes into the episode.

The last thing I think about before sleep takes me is Graham Adams and I hate that he's even on my mind at all.

GRAHAM

TWO

"I THINK it might be possible to die from lack of sex, which is actually ridiculous seeing as how I've got a whole contact list full of girls waiting to hook up."

Except, I'm superstitious as fuck, like most hockey players are, and I played the best game of my life after inadvertently cancelling my first Tuesday of the month sex appointment, which meant I had to see if it would last.

And it has.

Almost an entire month of no sex.

A month.

I'm skating faster and shooting the puck like a god. I'm un-fucking-touchable. Which means that, for now, I'm refraining from sex. I can't break this streak, so if I die… you know exactly why. And if I'm being honest, I'm over the hookups. It's beginning to get boring. There's nothing… memorable about them, and maybe that's what started this superstition anyway.

Who knows.

"You're the most dramatic *man* I've ever met," Reed grumbles as he scoops protein powder into his shaker.

What does a guy do when he's trying not to focus on the fact that he's been abstinent for the longest time since he lost his virginity? Well, he annoys the fuck out of his best friends.

Let's be real though, I'm here to see my Olive you and Evan. Not Reed. Not Briggs.

Briggs brought his daughter, my favorite girl in the world, over to Reed's, so we could all hang out. Evan, Reed's nephew that lives with him, is running around the house hitting us with nerf bullets at every turn.

The kid has crazy good aim, and I have a throbbing eyeball to prove it.

Shit.

Olive's in her high chair, demolishing the strawberry pancakes I just made us. I think there's some in her hair, which makes me chuckle because that means she's loving them. Seeing Olive is the best part of my day, hands down. Ever since she was born, we've had a special bond.

That's probably why they put up with my sorry ass. Because their kids love me.

But, it's true. The guys and their families are the only family I have here. My family is thousands of miles away on a small-ass farm in Tennessee and they only come to visit once, maybe twice a year. I make it there when I can, but my family here is what keeps me going.

Olive, Ev and my brothers.

"Eh, I know I'm dramatic. I own it, it makes me who I am." I shrug, a confident smirk on my face as I shovel another syrup-drenched pancake into my mouth. "Plus, you two keep me around so that's gotta count for something."

Briggs looks at me with a blank expression. "That's for Olive and Olive only."

Figures.

"You gotta clean this up before Holland and Maddison get home and kill us both. You know how Holl is about the kitchen."

"Mama home?" Olive says at the mention of Maddison. It's crazy how much she's talking now.

Briggs nods, plastering a wide grin on his face before walking over and picking pieces of pancake and strawberry out of her adorable pig tails or "piggies" as she calls them.

"That's right my girl, Mama and Auntie Holl will kick our butts if we don't clean up our mess. Speaking of mess… time for a bath. You've got syrup on your forehead. Reed, can I borrow your bathtub?"

Briggs holds her out like she's going to get syrup all over him.

Reed laughs and nods.

"Yay! I play with mermaids?" Olive asks.

He nods. "Of course." Turning toward me, he gestures toward the pile of dishes in the sink. "All yours."

Ugh. I love to cook, like more than most guys do, but I fucking hate dishes.

Bringing my plate over to the sink, I put it on top of the rest and get to work. Once the dishwasher's loaded, I look under the sink for pods, but come up empty.

Shit, this house has too many damn cabinets. Where do they keep anything? Holland insisted on ample storage Reed told me, but fuck, how do you keep track of everything.

I open the cabinet next to the pantry, and my eyes land on the clear bin full of dishwasher pods.

Bingo.

I grab one then shut the door, and in doing so, a piece of paper falls from the counter. Shit. Reaching down, I pick it up and flip it over.

What's this?

It's a list of names, numbered one to five.

"The hell?"

My brow furrows in confusion when I see my name, written in girly handwriting, next to number five.

Hm. I shove the list into the pocket of my gym shorts while I finish cleaning up our breakfast mess. I'm wiping the counter down when I hear the front door open, and Holland appears in the entryway with Maddison right behind her. Her long hair is tied up on the top of her head, and she's got a bright pink yoga mat tucked under her arm.

Seconds later, Emery follows behind them, wearing a black sports bra and a pair of leggings, clutching her own mat and a small gym bag.

"Graham." Holland smiles warmly, setting her gear down in the mudroom.

Maddison tosses me a quick wave, "Hey, have you seen Briggs and Olive?"

"Yep, they're in the bathtub. She had syrup on every surface of the kitchen, including herself."

"Not surprising in the least," Maddison laughs then disappears through the door and down the hallway.

Emery's eyes roll at the sight of me, which makes me smirk. Reed's little sister is a spitfire, and damn if she doesn't hate my guts, but the question is why? When we first met there was this undeniable chemistry, and while I still feel this attraction towards her, it's clear she isn't interested anymore, and I want to know why.

I want to know why, and I want her. She's hot. As fuck. Fun-sized, dark wavy hair that I want to wrap my fist around. Plump, kissable lips paired with blue eyes so stark against her dark hair that it disarms you at first glance. I've always had a thing for her… just in secret.

"Adams," she says, breezing past me toward the fridge. Her black manicured fingers wrap around the handle, swinging it open and grabbing a Fiji water. My eyes never leave hers as she uncaps it and brings it to her full rose-colored lips.

Fuck, I've got it bad for this girl, hating me and all. Maybe it's the lack of sex going to my brain, or maybe… it's because it's *her*.

"Why are you looking at me like that?" she asks, her nose scrunched.

I shrug. "Just observing."

"Observe somewhere else please and thank you."

"Emery!" Holland scoffs. "Don't be rude."

Emery rolls her eyes again, sets the water down on the counter, and smirks. "Aww, am I hurting your feelings, Graham?"

Sassy as fuck. Every time she talks, I want to put her over my knee and spank her until the only thing she can do is moan my name. She hates me, and I'd be lying if I said it didn't bother me. I've got zero clue as to why. I'm everyone's favorite, so why not her?

"Nah, but if you wanna make me feel better, I'm available."

"Please," she scoffs, "that's number one on my list of things I'll never be doing."

Speaking of lists…

I reach into my pocket and pull out the list of names I found while cleaning and hold it up between two fingers. "Holland, know anything about this list I found earlier? Has my name on it."

Holland looks confused and shakes her head. "No, I've

never seen it." She leans in closer, her eyes squinting. "Emery, is this yours? It looks like your handwriting."

My gaze whips to Emery, who suddenly looks nervous and has wide eyes. A second later, it's ripped from my hand, and she's crumpling it up and tossing it into the trash can.

Well, now my curiosity is really piqued. Obviously, she didn't want anyone to see that list or she wouldn't have reacted that way.

I cross my arms over my chest and grin. "What was that, Emery, and why am I number five on it?"

My questions are met with silence. Emery's lips are pursed in a flat, thin line as Holland looks back and forth between us.

"Wait, is that the scorecard you told me about while I was on vacation?"

"Jesus, Holland, SHUT UP," Emery cries, her cheeks red. She's obviously flustered.

"Scorecard?" I ask.

Holland covers her mouth in a giggle. "Oh, this is *good*. I wanna see how this plays out. Go on, Em, tell him what it means."

Emery shakes her head, crossing her arms across her chest. "Absolutely not."

"Yeah, Em, tell me what it is," I goad her, a smirk on my lips.

"No."

She tries to brush past me into the living room, but my hand wraps around the warm skin of her bicep, stopping her. "Tell me, or I'll ask Reed. I'm sure he'd love to know too if he doesn't already."

She groans, dropping her head back against her shoulders in frustration, staring up at the ceiling, and my eyes lower to the swell of her tits that are protruding from the top of the tight sports bra containing them. I pull my eyes away, before I get distracted by her fantastic rack, and focus back on the score-card, as Holland called it.

"Spill it, Davidson."

Her eyes narrow.

"It's a scorecard. Of the players we'd..." her voice lowers, "sleep with in order of looks and fuckability." She looks like it pained her to say it out loud to me, which makes it even better.

I shake my head and laugh. Until I realize...

I'm number five on Emery's fuckable scorecard. Last.

Fucking *LAST*.

What. The. Actual. Fuck?

"Wait, and I'm fucking *five*? That's last!" My eyes bulge. No fucking way did I come in after Hudson *and* Asher on this list.

At this point, I'm barely registering Holland laughing so hard behind us that she's doubled over on the counter.

I'm fucking flabbergasted, and you know what, quite fucking offended as well.

She shrugs. "Sorry."

Except she doesn't look sorry at all. If anything, she looks... pleased.

"So, you're saying, you'd sleep with Hudson and Asher before me?" You can hear the disbelief in my tone, and all she does is shrug again.

"Look, we drank a shit ton of Dom, and made the list for shits and giggles. I honestly wouldn't sleep with you, even if you were number one on that list, Graham." She smirks smugly, taunting me with her words.

Wow, cut me fucking deep, why don't you. Not that I haven't thought about fucking Emery Davidson before now, because I have. Many, many times. More times than I'd like to admit, since she's my best friend's little sister, and obviously would rather drink bleach than touch me.

But, if anything, it just made her hotter.

In a fucked-up way. Obviously, I need therapy, but I'm a 'Never Back Down from a Challenge' kind of guy.

And Emery Davidson is the best kind of challenge there is.

"Why'd you make it in the first place then, Em?" I step closer to her, slightly lowering my voice. I watch as her throat bobs, and she takes a small step back.

"Because we were drunk and stupid. It's just a stupid list. Don't take it seriously, Graham."

With that, she spins on her heel and leaves me standing there. My eyes never leave her as she gathers her bag and water bottle, drops a quick kiss on Holland's cheek and leaves.

I shake my head. "Number fucking five. Can you believe that shit?" I grumble all the way to the trash, where I fish the list off the top and unwrinkle it. Emery's feminine handwriting stares back at me.

"Did you seriously just get that out of the trash?" Holland asks.

"Hell yes, I did. I'm holding on to this. What's Emery's deal anyway? Why does she hate me so much?"

Holland pulls her lip between her teeth and looks down at the bottle in her hands before looking up at me. "I don't know, Graham. I just think she doesn't like guys who..."

"Guys who what?"

"You know guys who are players. She's been burnt pretty badly in the past."

I mull over her words. "So, because I like to fuck, she hates me?"

Reed chooses that moment to stroll back into the kitchen, Olive and Evan trailing behind him. "Language. And why are you talking about fucking with my wife." He whispers the word, 'fucking' to avoid Olive and Evan hearing.

Holland laughs and tells him what happened over the last few.

"And I'm sorry I asked. Graham, don't get any ideas. I'll have to rip your arms off and beat you to death with them."

Ignoring him, I walk over to Evan and offer him my fist. "Uncle G has to go but see you soon, okay bud?"

He nods and bumps my fist, then skips off, leaving the adults alone.

"I'm going to the gym," I tell them, then pick up the still slightly crinkled paper from the counter. "And I'm taking this with me."

Five.

Last on the damn scorecard.

Anything less than number one is a no-go for me.

There's lots of times where I don't mind coming last.

Like when I'm between a girl's thighs.

But five? With a face like this?

Nah.

You know what? Fuck no. I'm not accepting this. If Emery Davidson thinks I'm not even in the top three, I'll show her that I always come first, well... that is after she does.

Starting with my tongue, followed by my cock.

―――

My friends are dicks. Okay, not entirely true, but the fact that they're laughing like it's the funniest shit they've ever heard right now, makes them dicks.

"Stop fucking laughing." I grunt. "You three are assholes."

Asher, Hudson, Briggs and I have been skating all morning,

but I've only now told them the reason I've been in such a shit mood, after skating out my frustration all morning.

The fact that I'm in a shit mood is what brought the topic up in the first place. I'm *never* in a bad mood. I try to make the best out of everything. It's one of my best traits.

It's the reason they started to call me, Sunshine, when I was no longer a rookie.

"The fact that you're number five on that list, and that you're this upset about it is fucking hilarious man," Asher wheezes.

"Yeah, well, it's bullshit. That's what it is."

Leave it to Emery Davidson to be the first woman to ever bruise my ego.

"Guess you're no longer the fans' first choice, G, it's me now." Hudson beams, slapping me on the back of the head with his stick and using a little too much force.

"I hate you. All of you. Listen, I don't know how to process this kind of rejection. It stings, alright?"

Briggs rolls his eyes, skating a wide circle around me. "I think you'll survive. She's just one girl, plus, have you forgotten the most important part?"

My eyebrows rise.

"She's Reed's little sister and I'm pretty sure he'll cut your dick off and feed it to you if you as so much glance in her direction. You've got an entire contact list full of girls who will drop anything to sleep with you, Graham. One girl rejecting you, isn't going to wound your ego for life."

It's the principle of it, though.

Now, I want to fucking prove her wrong.

Even if Reed does kill me. He can bury me with my pride.

"Yeah, well, now I have to show her why I'm number one," I tell them.

Hudson and Asher shake their heads while Briggs groans.

"Aren't you on some kind of sex ban anyway?" Hudson says.

"Yup. I'm a born-again virgin. That is until my streak is over." I shrug. "Don't judge me. It's the same reason you wear three pairs of socks, Hudson, and you," I point at Asher, "hit the ice three times with your stick before you're on it. Everyone has their shit."

Asher holds his hands up in surrender. "I'm not judging your superstition, bro. But I am judging you for being so butt hurt over that list. Like Briggs said, she's *one* girl. That you have a better chance of getting struck by lightning than ever touching."

Fuck.

They're right. But they also don't know that I've had a hard-on for Emery and that mouth of hers since the first day I met her. Back then… I thought maybe I had it in the bag, and then one day, she just stopped smiling at me and turned her nose up when I was around. I've always had a thing for her, and she's never given me the time of day.

It's fucked with me since. What made her hate me? Why the sudden switch? All I know is one thing's for certain. I'm going to change her mind, no matter what it takes. By the time I'm done, that number one spot will be mine.

EMERY

THREE

"HEY, Emery, can I talk to you in my office for a second?" My boss, Rob, pops his head around the corner of my cubicle. Shit. I hope I didn't forget something.

First-year associates always take the flack; something I've been learning rather quickly. There's a level of hierarchy at a firm this size, and aside from interns, I'm at the bottom. I'm the one who's going to sit and pour over files for hours, long after everyone else has gone home. At this stage, I'm a glorified researcher/assistant. Yes, the senior partners have asked me to get them coffee. More than once.

Not that I'm complaining because I'm living my dream. Being an attorney is all I can ever remember hoping to be, and now I am. I just have to work hard, and I'll earn my spot on that wall with the other partners.

Ever since I was a little girl, I knew that I wanted to be an attorney. I'd put on my mom's old high heels and prance around the house with a stack of books that was almost as tall as I was, pretending I was working on my next best case. There's never been hesitation or doubt about my future, about what career I wanted to pursue.

"Yes, of course," I say quickly, standing from my chair and smoothing down my black pencil skirt.

Following behind him, I walk into his massive, luxury office that only senior partners are afforded. The furniture is all dark mahogany wood. Sleek and masculine.

"Have a seat." He gestures from the other side of his desk.

I swallow nervously, adjusting my skirt to sit in the wide chair opposite of him.

When he doesn't immediately say anything, my nerves only intensify.

"I called you in here to talk because we're hoping to take on a big case in the near future. A new client has reached out to us that would be game changing for this firm."

I nod.

I watch as his fingers, one adorned with a gold wedding band, hover over the thick file on his desk.

"You're a first-year associate, but you've got promise, Emery. You're smart, cunning, and ambitious. Which is exactly what this firm needs, and even though you're only starting out, I can tell your future is going to be bright. I've known even when you were still an intern that you were going places."

My cheeks warm under his praise, but I manage to squeak out, "Thank you."

Normally, I'm a confident girl. Overly confident sometimes. But when it comes to the senior partners, I'm all nerves. They have my career in the palm of their hands, and just as easily as they brought me in, can have me out the door. Years of interning and hard work out the window.

Just like that.

So, I do my best to fly under the radar, putting my head down and getting the job done. Efficiently and diligently.

"I want you and Camden working with this client. He hasn't agreed to use our firm yet, and he's a close friend of both my wife and I, so he's granted us the opportunity to sit down and speak with him. He's a philanthropist and investor here in Chicago."

"And you want me to work on his case?" I ask in disbelief.

He laughs haughtily. "Yes, with Brandon's assistance." A junior partner.

But still. Holy shit. Being given the opportunity to work on a client of this caliber… it's amazing. Unbelievable really.

"Thank you so much…for even considering me. I'm in shock."

"You earned it. Now, the meeting isn't going to be for another month and a half or so because of his prior commitments, but I wanted to bring you in and get you up to speed on the information that we have, so when it's time, you can jump right in. We want to impress him with our knowledge, Emery."

I nod. "Understandable. I won't let you down, Rob. Thank you again."

He nods and stands, extending his hand, which I quickly shake, praying he doesn't feel how clammy my palm is in his. I exit his office, holding in the squeal until I'm back at my desk.

Wow, so not what I was expecting when Rob asked to talk to me.

I sit in my chair and immediately pull out my phone, firing off a quick text to the girls, saying celebratory drinks are needed. Stat. My phone vibrates with their responses, and I smile.

This is exactly what I needed to take my mind off the one

person it shouldn't be on, the same one who's been infiltrating my thoughts since our run-in at Holland's.

The Avalanches' very own playboy has been keeping me up for the past three nights against my will. He's taken my mind hostage, and I'm even more annoyed at him for it. Partly because of the way he stepped closer to me, lowering his voice to a hoarse, raspy whisper in Holland's kitchen, causing my core to tingle.

The traitor.

Bringing those old feelings back to the surface, even though I've pushed them down for as long as I can remember.

And partly because of the text that came through two days later.

I've read it at least fifty times, but now I'm doing my best to ignore it and pretend it isn't there.

It's entirely inappropriate, and he's a dick for sending it.

A dick that makes my thighs clench together.

My finger hovers over the message with his unsaved number, as I decide whether or not to read it again. I press the message and my eyes scan it once more.

I might be number five on your scorecard, but if you give me one night, I'll give you ten reasons why I should be number one, and I don't even need to use my cock.

The word 'cock' coming from Graham Adam's lips seems even more dirty when I try to imagine it. Which I am, imagining it now that it's on my phone.

See? Wholly inappropriate.

What was he thinking?!

"Emery?"

A deep voice startles me, causing my phone to fly from my hand and bounce against my computer screen before falling with a loud thump against my desk.

"Yes, I'm s-sorry," I stutter, standing quickly and straightening my blouse before turning around to face him.

It's Brandon, the junior partner from the fourth floor. I've only met him twice since, most of the time, I do my best to stay out of senior partner's way and keep to my cubicle unless needed. He's wearing a dark navy suit, paired with a red tie. He's probably about ten years older than me, and has dark, chestnut brown hair. He's an attractive guy, but that's not what makes me nervous. It's the fact that in this case? He's practically my boss.

He laughs and extends his hand. "Hi."

I slide my palm in his and plaster on a bright smile. "Hi. Sorry, I was checking some emails on my phone."

"No problem. I just wanted to come down and say congratulations on being chosen for the Monterrey case. I'm happy that we'll be working together."

"Me too. Honestly? I can't believe it, but I'm excited, and I'm going to work really hard."

I'm rambling because I'm nervous. *Get it together, Emery. This is nothing. You are a strong, independent, badass bitch.*

"Great, well, if you're free this afternoon, I can sit with you and go over what we have?"

I nod. "That would be great. Thank you."

He smiles warmly then nods, and then turns on his heel and is gone. I quickly pick up my phone and send a text back to the girls.

Going to need that drink sooner rather than later. Tonight? 7 @ Lush Library.

Placing my phone back in my desk drawer, I open my web browser then get a new notebook and begin reading anything and everything I can about Zack Monterrey.

All while trying not to think about the text on my phone or about anything that deals with Graham Adams at all.

The rest of the day passes in a blur of meetings and so much information that my head spins. I don't make it to Lush Library until after seven thirty, and when I walk through the door, I spot Lea, Ana and Holland at a table in the far back corner, drinks already in front of them.

My heels click against the concrete as I walk to the booth, then flop into the seat next to Holland. Lea and Ana are both sipping their drinks when I sit down.

"Longest day ever. *Need* margaritas," I mutter, rubbing my temples with my fingers to ease the headache that formed hours ago.

Holland laughs and pushes the strawberry margarita, my favorite, across the table toward me.

"Tell us everything."

I start by telling them about the new case I got handed to me today, and how the client is someone big and that we aren't able to discuss much about it outside the firm.

"It's just unreal, guys, this rarely ever happens. Especially to first-year associates. If I want to make a name at this firm, this is the time to do it. This will put me on the map. Basically, we have to schmooze the client, tell them everything they want to hear, be everything they want, for them to choose our firm and from the sound of it, not landing them is not an option."

Holland leans over, wrapping her arm around my stress-tightened shoulders. "Listen, you are Emery Davidson, the baddest, most stubborn and hardworking bitch that I know. You've got this in the bag, no question."

I nod, not entirely convinced.

Thank God I've got my girls and this drink to distract me. The margarita is strong and sweet. Exactly how I love it. My tongue slides along the rim, licking the bitter salt as the tequila slides down my throat with ease.

"I needed this too," Lea says, "I'm a glorified assistant at the firm I'm at."

My lips tug into a sympathetic frown. I get it. I totally do. "It's going to pay off, Lee, don't worry. We work our way up the ladder, and then five years from now, when we're on our way to being junior partners and rich, we'll look back and say this was nothing."

Ana nods. She's not a lawyer, but a pediatric nurse at the hospital. She specializes in working with NICU babies. Specifically, babies that are born prematurely. We met at the library for the first time, and the rest was history. She became a part of our girl gang.

"Not to rain on everyone's parade but…" Holland looks at me with her nose crinkled. "Reed and the guys are coming."

"Holl," I groan into my margarita.

"I'm sorry, I know, I know, but your mom has Evan tonight for a sleepover, and he and the guys were at home playing Xbox or something, so I was trying to be nice offering them to come. Honestly, I didn't think they'd take me up on that offer, but they did."

Great. Hockey players travel in packs, so I'm sure that means that my least favorite person will be coming too.

"Oooh is Hudson coming?" Ana wiggles her eyebrows suggestively.

"You are out of control." I laugh. "It's fine, we'll do girls' night soon. I'm not going to stay late anyway; I have to be at work at five tomorrow if I want to impress Brandon."

"Who's Brandon?" Lea asks.

"The junior partner I'm assigned with on this case. He's really nice. We went over all the material we have and agreed to meet back tomorrow to handle the rest." I drain the rest of my margarita and lick the salt from my lip. "One more drink."

Famous last words.

I've spent the last hour taking shots with my brother, who insisted he owed me for being out of town when I celebrated passing the Bar. He obviously didn't owe me anything, seeing as how he bought me a brand-new iMac, MacBook and iPad as a graduation present, but who am I to pass up free top-shelf tequila?

Not to mention that now I have to endure sitting at the same booth as Graham Adams, who my brother, of course, brought with him. And of course, he looks even sexier than the last time I saw him.

That asshole.

His perfect tousled hair, and ridiculously attractive dimples.

"No more." I groan. "I'm going to puke."

Reed laughs, deep and loud, and it echoes off the walls of the small bar, even over the music. "C'mon, you used to be a champ."

"Yeah, well, age does that to you. I'm not going to be able to move tomorrow."

Shit, tomorrow. I have to work. Why in the hell did I do all of those shots?

I was peer-pressured.

And because I've spent the better part of the night ignoring Graham, I distracted myself with said shots. Even after all of this tequila, I'm still trying to avoid his eyes at all costs.

My head feels heavy, and the room in front of me seems a tad bit fuzzy, but at least I feel good. Buzzed, relaxed. Happy to be with all the people I love, even though the guys crashed our girls' night.

Suddenly, my phone sounds, and when I glance down, I see it's my boss.

Shit. Shit. Shit.

I am waaaaayyyyy too drunk to talk to him.

"Guys, I need to step outside. It's Rob. I'll be back," I mutter, glancing around the table, Graham's honey flecked eyes locking on mine.

I tear my gaze from his and walk out of the bar onto the sidewalk, assaulted by the cold night air. My finger swipes across the screen, answering Rob's call.

"Hi!" I say cheerfully, or what I hope is at least cheerful, probably just overenthusiastic.

"Hi Emery, I'm sorry to call you this late, but I just wanted to let you know that I'll be out of the office this week. Something's come up and I need you to do me a favor."

He's calling me for favors now?

"Can you go over the contract for the Arrow case? I feel like something is off, and I want to take another thorough look at it before we go to the deposition."

"Yes, of course," I say quickly. "That's no problem."

I hear shuffling in the background, and a car door slam. "Thanks, I'm headed out now, but if you find anything incorrect in the contract then make those adjustments and email it over to me, and make sure to CC Nate on them."

Nate is another senior partner in the firm that I avoid at all costs because he's intimidating as fuck.

"Got it," I squeak.

"Thanks Emery. Have a great night."

"You too, sir."

I end the call and expel the breath I was holding, my lungs sucking in fresh air as I groan.

That contract is easily eighty pages long.

I guess I'll be working till ten p.m. tomorrow. Speaking of the time, I glance down at my phone and see that it's close to midnight. Shit.

"Kinda cold out here, huh, Davidson?"

His voice startles me, but I show no reaction. I look up and see Graham standing a few feet away, leaning against the brick side of the bar.

"Obviously so, Adams. Having trouble reading the forecast?" I retort, crossing my arms over my chest.

His grin hits me directly in the gut, causing my stomach to swirl and tighten. His teeth are white and straight, and his smile, well...they call him 'Sunshine' for a reason. He pushes back off the wall and steps closer, causing my heart to go haywire.

No, no.

No.

This is the worst idea.

Actually, no. It's not an idea at all. I'm just drunk, and... horny. And thinking thoughts I really should not be.

Jesus, why are his muscles so... thick and so... *ugh*.

"What's that look for?" he asks, coming to a halt directly in front of me, so close our breath mingles between us. I can nearly taste the whiskey on his breath.

I swallow thickly, wishing my brain wasn't so fuzzy from

the alcohol, and the fact that he smells so good. Delicious. All man, cedar and spice.

Stop it, Emery. Graham Adams is the very last thing, literally on the planet, that you should be attracted to. Tequila shots or not.

"Oh, just me wishing that you'd suddenly disappear back through that door you came in." I clench my teeth, taking a step back, putting distance between us.

Graham laughs. A deep and low rumble that I feel in the pit of my stomach. "You know the 'hard to get' thing just makes me want it more, right?"

My eyes roll. Of course, it does. Except I'm not "playing hard to get" because I'm not playing at all.

"You're delusional."

He shrugs, stepping closer. "I hear what you're saying Emery. But the thing is, you can say it all day long, but your body shows me everything I need to know." Reaching out, he runs his finger gently along the column of my throat, pausing right where my pulse beats wildly. "I told you to give me one night. One night to prove to you why I deserve that number one spot."

"It's just a stupid list, why is it bothering you so badly?

"Because since the second I laid eyes on you, all I've wanted to do is put you beneath me and fuck you until you trembled. So, hearing I scored so low on your "list" was a shock to my ego. One I want to fucking rectify." He stares at me through heavy-lidded, desire-filled eyes, daring me with just his lingering gaze and the heat his body radiates.

Suddenly, my tongue feels heavy, and I'm too stunned to speak. I mean, yeah… at first maybe we flirted a little until I realized how much of a manwhore douchebag he is. But hearing those dirty words from his mouth hits differently.

"I don't even like you, Graham, why would I want to sleep with you? Be another one of your bunnies that you collect on each day of the week? No thanks. Not interested." I look down at my newly painted nails, feigning boredom.

He steps closer, forcing me backward until my back collides with the cold brick of the bar. I feel him everywhere, on every exposed piece of skin on my body while his fingers still only rest on my throat. His eyes darken, desire ghosting through them.

"Don't have to like each other for me to make you come, Emery." He smirks, taunting me, slowly dragging his fingers lower until they rest on my collar bone, under my now heaving chest.

Fuck, this is bad. This is *so so* bad.

Leaning down, his lips brush against the shell of my ear, sending a hard shiver down my spine. His hot breath fans my ear as he rasps, "One night. That's all I need."

The fact that I'm even considering this shows that drunk Emery obviously makes very bad decisions, but... I'd be lying if I said my thighs didn't clench together at his closeness.

I squeeze my eyes shut, sucking in a gulp of air, trying to keep my thoughts straight, but it's too late. Graham has infiltrated them, and slowly, I feel my resolve lessening. When his fingers brush against my nipples, I shudder, unable to control my reaction to his touch.

Would one night really be *that* bad?

My eyes pop open to find him staring at me intently, lust burning in his irises. The very same feeling that's coursing through my head, making it fuzzy. When his hands slide down my waist, and his fingers slip under my shirt to stroke my side, my restraint is gone.

Poof. Goodbye bitch. Drunk Emery is a raging horny ho, and apparently that means having sex with people you despise. Honestly, it's not my fault. Even though he's the world's biggest douchebag, he's also hot as fuck and a girl is only so strong. I only have *so* much will power and it's being offered so graciously.

His gaze lands on mine, our eyes locking in a feverish moment that heats me from the inside out. It feels like he could devour me in one single bite.

It's hot, and my thighs tremble as I take a shaky breath, swallowing down my trepidations.

We collide together in a frenzy, his hands sliding down to my ass to hoist me up against the brick wall. Finally, god, *finally,* his lips are on mine and he's kissing me. I'm not surprised that the man kisses like a god, causing butterflies to erupt in my stomach, but I am surprised how much *I* like it.

One taste and I'm desperate for more.

Graham rips his lips from mine and stares back at me as we both pant. "Wait, wait... we should talk about this or something."

"Stop talking. Please. For the love of God. *Stop. Talking.*" With my hands still wrapped around his neck, I pull him back toward me and seal my lips over his, silencing him.

If I stop to think about what I'm actually doing, I'll come to my senses, and right now, I want to be blissfully ignorant. We don't *actually* have to like each other to have sex. We're two consenting adults who had lots of tequila to blame their bad decisions on. Well, not so much tequila that I don't know what's happening.

His hand travels higher and higher until it slips beneath the cup of my bra. When his fingers make contact with the bare skin of my nipple, I suck in a hiss against his lips.

For this being the worst idea I've ever had, it feels entirely too right.

So right that I'm blaming my inner sex-fiend succubus as I tear my lips from his and whisper, "Take me home. Now."

For once, Graham doesn't argue, and I'm back on my feet as he drags me the two blocks to my house.

GRAHAM

FOUR

OF ALL THE ways I thought this night would end, this is not it. Not even close. I thought I was going to drink a little with the guys, then head home. But the night took a turn with Reed and the guys ordering round and round of shots, and then, the next thing I knew, I was dry-humping Emery against the wall outside of the bar.

Emery fucking Davidson.

Goddamn, I must be dead and this is heaven. Surely as fuck, this can't be real. Honestly, heaven comes in the form of a short brunette that would bust my balls in a split second. That shit does it for me.

Well... Emery does it for me. Which is fucking dumb, seeing as how her brother will have my nuts in a jar for even looking at her. Actually, that's wrong.

Emery will have my nuts in a jar for even *looking* at her. Except, I must have entered the pearly white gates, and she's my gift from the big man upstairs since I'm practically a born-again virgin. My vow of celibacy and all.

Clumsily, she tries putting the key into the lock on her front door but keeps missing the keyhole. When I close my hand over hers and take the jangling keys from her, her ocean blue eyes connect with mine, and she pounces on me, causing the keys to fall to the floor with a loud clink.

Her hands thread in the strands of my too long hair, and she pants against my lips as her tongue battles with mine. I feel her moan all the way to my cock.

We're basically fucking with our clothes on against her front door, and I sincerely hope I don't have to come face to face with her neighbors. Reaching down, I hoist her up as her legs lock around my waist.

"Keys," she mumbles against my lips, never fully taking hers off mine. Without pausing, I hold onto her by her ass and squat down, blindly reaching for them. Fuck, the hallway spins as I bend down, the whiskey going straight to my head, but I somehow manage to pick them up. When I get a firm grip on the keys, she breaks the kiss, to point out the right one, and I easily open the door, taking us inside.

It's not the first time I've been inside her house, since the guys and I helped her move in, but it's the first time I've been inside with her pussy against my cock and her lips against my neck.

Using my foot, I slam the door shut and toss the keys somewhere on the floor. I'm scared if I stop, she'll start to overthink the situation and I don't want this to fucking end.

Not when it's just getting started. Not when I'm so close to being able to finally fucking have her.

I feel her hand reach between us, hiking her skirt up, revealing a smooth plane of black silk that has my mouth literally watering. Fuck, I want to taste her. I want to fuck her until the only name she can moan is mine, until she's falling apart around my dick. Glancing up, I catch her gaze, and she groans, "Touch me."

A plea. She's as desperate as I feel.

Happily, I oblige, my fingers sliding across her pussy, the silk beneath my fingertips feeling like the softest, most erotic thing I've ever touched.

I can feel how wet she is, and I'm not pausing. Not letting this spell we're under to break. I wrap the flimsy material around my fingers and pull, tearing it free from her body. She yelps, squirming against the tent of my pants.

"God damnit Graham."

"What?" I'm still clutching the tattered silk.

Her lips find mine again in an urgent kiss, but she pulls back. "Those were expensive as fuck, but that was so hot."

I smirk and run my thumb along the seam of her pussy, dipping inside her slightly. My eyes never leave her as she drops her head backward and moans.

It's the best sound in the goddamn world.

My thumb brushes along her clit lightly, and she arches against my fingers, begging, *"More."*

I slide two fingers inside her, cursing inwardly with how tight she is, knowing I'm not going to last long once I'm inside of her. Say what you want, but there's not a fucking chance.

I'm already about to come in my pants like a fucking teenager with how badly I want her.

Pressing her back against the door, I fuck her with my fingers, slow and unhurried, until she's squirming in my arms. She's a panting mess as she tries to hold on, climbing higher and higher.

"Fuck me." She moans against my ear as she rides my fingers.

"You sure?"

She nods adamantly, reaching between us to palm my cock through my jeans. "Now." Her fingers fumble with the button of my jeans, popping it free, then tugs my zipper down.

I don't actually want to fuck her against the front door, but neither of us seem to want to pause to make it to another surface in her house. I want to lie her down and spend the rest of the night fucking her into oblivion.

Those thoughts are out the window as I feel her hand circle my cock and give it a rough pull.

My eyes roll back, and I stop thinking of anything but Emery. My fingers are still wet from her pussy, so I bring them to my mouth and suck the taste of her off of my fingers, grinning around them when her eyes go wide.

For a moment, she pauses, but then like a fire, she burns brighter, pulling my fingers from my mouth, and slamming her lips against mine. I know she can taste herself, and it only seems to make her squirm more. She's pressed against my cock, her wetness coating me, and I almost lose it.

Almost.

"Emery," I groan, pressing her harder against the door. "You're fucking killing me." Wrenching the hot pink top she's wearing up, I pull the cups of her bra down, letting her ample tits spill free.

If there was ever perfection, actual unflawed perfection to exist on earth, I'm convinced it's perched on my dick right now.

Truly, I fucking believe it.

Emery Davidson is perfection. Her hips wide, and perfect for me to hold. Supple tits, an ass that leaves me at a loss for words.

I'm practically fucking drooling.

"Fuck me, Graham," she begs, writhing against me, reaching for my cock again, and this time, she presses down with my head inside her. We both hiss when she slides down an inch, sheathing herself.

God damnit, she feels incredible, un-fucking-believable. My hands travel down to her ass as I roll my hips. Torturously slow. Her lips are on my neck, her hands under my t-shirt, scraping down my back as I grind upwards, rubbing her clit in the process, bottoming out.

I swear to God I see fucking stars. *Actual fucking stars.*

"Jesus," I groan, gripping her hips harder as I stand still. I can't let this be over yet. Not a chance.

"Move," she begs, rotating her hips back and forth.

"Unless you want this to be over before it starts, please for the love of God be still, Emery."

Did Emery just fucking giggle?

I've never heard her giggle in my life and now she's giggling about my lack of self-control.

"Wow, I think you just bruised my ego."

My hands flex on her ass as I pull out slowly, then thrust back in, harder this time, pushing her up against the door.

"Impossible. It's made of steel. Stop talking."

I groan when I feel her contract around me, knowing she's getting off on the fact that she has this effect on me.

Nah, if this is the only time that I get with her, I have to make it fucking count.

Especially when it's been a fantasy for far too fucking long. If I ever want it to happen again, I have to make her crazy for my dick.

My hand leaves her ass and travels up to the back of her neck where I grip her tight, forcing her to look up at me with wide eyes. "That mouth. I'm going to fuck that attitude right out of you, Davidson."

Her eyes dilate, flaming with desire. "You can try."

And try I fucking will. Pulling out of her almost completely, until the tip of my cock is barely inside her, I begin fucking her in earnest. Hard, deep thrusts that send bolts of pleasure down my spine. Over and over, I pound inside her, gripping her neck as she thrusts in my arms.

It's rough, sloppy, desperate, and everything I'd dreamed it to fucking be and more.

"I'm... I-I'm going to come." She moans. Her rosy, pink lips are bruised from our kisses, her hair is damp and plastered to her forehead, and her cheeks are flushed red. She's never looked more beautiful. Especially with the burn of my beard on her neck.

It makes me want to see the burn along her thighs.

Using my free hand, I drop my thumb to her clit and rub in sync with my thrusts, my eyes never leaving hers as the sound of our skin slapping fills the room, mixed with the breathless moans that tumble from her lips.

Moments later, she comes on my cock. Tightening, she writhes, her back arched in pleasure as I suck her nipple into my mouth.

"Graham, oh God." She cries, pulling at my hair as she detonates. I can't help but follow behind her, thrusting deep and succumbing to the pleasure. Slowly, I come back down to earth, my hips moving slightly until the movement is too much. Her head is buried in the column of my throat, her hot pants fanning along my neck. We're a sweaty fucking mess, and I just fucked the shit out of her against the door, but god damnit, it was perfect.

"Fuck, fuck. Shit," she says, her body suddenly tight with tension. I pull back and my eyebrows furrow.

"Not exactly what a guy likes to hear after his best performance..." I joke.

She shakes her head fervently. "Graham, we didn't use a condom!"

I freeze.

What in the fuck?

Glancing down, I look at where I'm still buried inside her, and sure enough.... I see my cum leaking out of her onto my dick.

While it's a bit alarming that we were so desperate that neither of us thought of protection, it's the hottest fucking thing I've ever seen.

I've never had sex without a condom, ever, not in my entire life. I'd be lying if I didn't say that my dick was beginning to stir back to life at the sight. There's something addictive about the sight of me dripping out of her. Makes me fucking crazy.

Irrationally so.

"I'm sorry, Em, I was so caught up in the moment." I pull out of her and set her on her feet, tucking myself back inside my boxers.

She rights herself, pulling her skirt back down, and shakes her head. "I'm on birth control... are you... clean?"

"Of course, I am, I can get you the paperwork from the team."

"No, no, I believe you. I am too." She pauses, looking around the room, avoiding my eyes. "So... we're good."

I nod. "Good."

She brushes past me into the living room, making a beeline for the kitchen, then opens the fridge and pulls out a carton of orange juice and begins to drink directly from it.

When she bends over to place it back in the fridge, I get a peek of her pussy, and now I am fully hard again.

I can't fucking help it; she's so goddamn hot, all self-control is lost when I look at her. I can't tell you how many times I dreamed of what it would be like to fuck this girl.

To have her just for one night, and now that's a reality.

And I'm sure as shit taking advantage of it.

"Davidson," I call her name, walking into the living room. She glances up before crossing her arms across her chest. "What?"

"C'mere."

She shakes her head. "Look... This was a mistake. I shouldn't... we shouldn't have done this. You're on my brother's team, and honestly, I don't even like you."

Wow, talk about brutal honesty.

I shrug. "Don't care. You and I both know that was hot as fuck, and I'm not done. Come. Here. Davidson."

When she doesn't move, I cross the living room and stop in front of her, grasping her jaw in both hands and leaning down before she can stop me, kissing her. Pulling back, I grin, "We can pretend it didn't happen tomorrow, if that's what you want, but for now... get your fine ass in that room because I'm nowhere near fucking done with you."

For a second, she pauses, and I think she might toss me out on my ass, but after a moment, she turns on her heel toward the bedroom, and I reach out and slap her ass.

Yelping, she narrows her eyes at me, but behind the bravado... I see it turns her on, and if I have my way, her ass will be red by the end of the night.

I wasn't joking when I said I was only getting started.

I've got one night, and I'm going to make it count.

EMERY

FIVE

JESUS, my head hurts. It seems to pound with each beat of my heart. The backs of my eyelids are a bit too bright, seeing as how I have blackout curtains in my house. Cracking one eye open, I peer around my room, trying to wake up from the fog of sleep and the heavy amount of alcohol I consumed last night. I groan when I see that my curtains are, indeed, open, letting the morning sunlight shine into the room.

Tossing my arm over my eyes, I feel the brush of my sheets against my nipples, and when I glance down, I realize that I'm completely naked, and there are.... Purplish blue marks scattered across my thighs and chest.

Oh god.

Last night comes flooding back in a wave of... *Oh my god.*

I had sex with Graham Adams. My body feels achy and sated, which only happens after a night of great sex.

Shit. This is so bad. How much tequila did I actually drink?

It's not that I can't remember; it's just that I really, *really* don't want to. Groaning again, I flip over and bury my face in my pillow, smelling a trace of the same cedar clean smell that is Graham, which proceeds to make me scream into the fabric.

Out of all the drunken mistakes I could have made.... *Graham Adams?*

After wallowing in self-pity for a few minutes, I drag myself from the bed and throw on a pair of underwear and a hoodie before heading straight for the kitchen.

I need Advil and coffee. Stat.

But I stop dead in my tracks when I round the corner into my kitchen. Why do you ask? Because the very person I was dreading facing again is standing in front of my stove, shirtless, with a pair of jeans slung low on his hips. The dimples in his back show right above the waistband, and the sense of dread in my stomach seems to change into something... different.... as my eyes travel up his back. The corded muscles of his back seem to ripple each time he flips the spatula.

The fucker is whistling.

Whistling.

"Please tell me I'm still drunk and hallucinating." I groan. My feet are still glued to the cold tile of the kitchen floor. "*Why* are you *still* here?"

Graham looks up and tosses me a boyish smirk. "I should've known you'd be a morning delight, Davidson, but never fear. My grandma's world-famous pancakes will make it all better."

Trudging over to the barstool at the island, I plop down. "No, what would make it all better is if you were like a normal guy and snuck out in the middle of the night. But, I obviously am not that lucky."

He laughs, turning his back toward me once more.

This is unreal. Why couldn't he be like a normal guy and be down for a drunken one-night stand that meant nothing? No, he has to stay for breakfast like he has nothing better to do.

Oh fuck.

"Fuck, fuck, fuck, what time is it?" I scramble out of the chair toward my room. In my hungover haze, I didn't even think to check the time. I'm probably late for work. I sprint to my room and straight to my closet. I'm sifting through my clothes, when I feel Graham's body against my back.

"Chill, you're not late." His breath fans out against my neck, causing me to shiver. I feel slightly better that I'm not late, but the fact that Graham is still in my house has to be dealt with. Immediately.

I whip around to face him, a small smile tugging at the corner of his lips, almost causing me to forget what it is that I need to say. "Okay, listen. We got drunk, we had hot, yet average sex. A couple of times."

He gasps out loud dramatically. "That's fucking offensive, Davidson, and you're a liar."

I shrug, and even though I *am* lying through my teeth, I continue, "Of course you'd be the clingy type. Listen… Graham. This was a mistake; you and I both know it."

His jaw steels, and the muscle along the carved expanse seems to ripple. "It was not a mistake. Just because you're not willing to face the truth, doesn't mean I am. I told you I needed one night to change your mind, and you're sitting here acting like you didn't come four times."

Swallowing thickly, I gulp down the acidic taste of my lies on my tongue. Fine.

Sex with Graham was fucking amazing, and even though it physically pains me to admit it, he has the dick of a god. I'd never come so many times from sex. I've only ever been able to bring myself to orgasm so effortlessly, well, until Graham walked in the picture.

But the fact is, this was a one-time thing, and there won't

59

ever be another time. Period. I don't even like Graham. Last night was a momentary lapse in judgment.

I need to put distance between us and get ready for work.

Before I can even speak, though, he's squatting down and throwing me, literally, over his shoulder.

I squeak in protest. "Oh my god, you caveman, put me down!" His shoulders shake beneath me, and then there's a loud, stinging slap directly on the bare flesh of my ass.

"If this is the last time that I get to taste your sweet pussy, I want you to admit that I'm number one on that list."

He tosses me down on the bed, where I slide up the mattress with how rough he throws me. My mind flashes back to last night and all of the ways he flung me around, so effortlessly, only to slide back inside me with so much force I felt it in my toes.

When I look up, his eyes are on me, and they darken. "What's that look for Emery?" He rasps, sending the butterflies in my stomach haywire.

God, what am I doing?

Why do I keep ending up under him?

"Annoyance. I have to be at work in an hour and I haven't even had a chance to shower. Like I said, it was fun, but you've overstayed your welcome."

Ignoring me, he drops to his knees and hooks his arms around my thighs, dragging me to the edge of the bed, and before I even have the chance to protest, he's pulling the thin fabric of my underwear aside and sealing his mouth over my clit.

I decide to shut up for five seconds, because Graham's mouth feels entirely too good to argue. One more time won't hurt....

Right?

My hands fly to his hair and my body arches against his lips when he sucks my clit into his mouth.

"Oh," I moan, tugging on his hair. It's longer than it usually is and right now, I'm thankful.

"Do you want to come, Emery?"

My eyes dart down to where he's kneeling between my thighs, currently sucking the sensitive flesh into his mouth, admiring the red, angry marks he's leaving behind on my pale skin.

Pulling my lip between my teeth, I bite down roughly, trying to hold back the moan that threatens to escape as he bites down on my thigh, rougher than before.

It's so hot, the feel of his rough stubble against my skin, his hot breath fanned out against my flesh. Hooking his thumbs in the waistband of my panties, he drags them down my legs and tosses them aside, never breaking our gaze.

Graham feasting on me like a starved man from below while looking up at me with every stroke of his tongue. I've never had anything feel so... dirty, and erotic. Leaning up on my elbows, I watch his movements as he parts me with his fingers and drinks in the sight.

"You have the prettiest pussy I've ever seen." His praise makes the anticipation even more torturous. "I could eat it all fucking day and never get tired of being between your thighs."

He then flicks his tongue against my clit, over and over until I'm a squirming, sloppy mess on my bed. My fingers grasp at the sheets so hard that my hands ache from holding them so tightly as he eats me. His tongue flattens over my clit over and over while he fucks me with his fingers, finding my G-spot effortlessly.

I may hate Graham, and I might be actually insane for falling into bed with the last man I ever should, but one thing is for certain... The man is a sex god. The rumors are actually true. It's the only rational explanation as to why I've lost my mind and ended up beneath him.

Despite my fiery dislike for him, my wanton need seems to burn brighter. So bright that I'm going to combust at any moment. He senses how close I am, because he closes his mouth over my clit and sucks, hard, scraping his teeth against the sensitive nub. My back leaves the bed, my hands fly to his hair and then... I fall.

Into the most blinding pleasure I've ever experienced. With only one night together, he somehow manipulates my body better than anyone ever before. He slides his rough, calloused hand up my body and tweaks my nipple between his fingers, tugging roughly, sending me even further into an ecstasy spiral.

My entire body is on fire for Graham.

Before I can even blink, he's folding his body over mine and thrusting deep, the aftershocks of my orgasm still present and blinding, and for the next thirty minutes, he doesn't let my mind wander.

He makes it impossible to do anything but focus on him and the things he's doing to my body.

By the time I make it to work, I'm flustered, and there's still an undeniable ache between my thighs that serves as a constant, annoying reminder of what happened last night... and this morning. Of the *mistakes* that transpired.

I knew from the moment his lips were on mine that sleeping with Graham would be a mistake, a huge one that could fuck absolutely everything up. And that knowledge makes it even worse today since I consciously made the decision to screw everything up by thinking with my vagina.

Ugh.

My phone vibrates against the metal of my desk drawer, pulling me from my work that I'm not actually focusing on at the moment. Sliding it out, I open the text notification and see it's from Graham.

Shaking my head, I scan the message.

Graham: Still thinking about my cock Davidson?

I groan, dropping my head to my desk and trying to ignore the feeling of dread in my stomach. I allow myself a brief moment of pity before I type a hasty response.

Me: Actually, the opposite. Trying to burn the memory from my brain. Why are you even texting me?

Graham: So grumpy for someone who got their brains fucked out all night. Need a repeat already?

What? No! My thumbs tap at my screen with more force than necessary, making the loud tapping of my fingers, echo around the walls of my cubicle. How can someone so... infuriating cause so many emotions to simmer inside me at the same time?

Jesus, this is getting worse by the second.

Me: You're insane, and obviously have trouble taking a hint. This was a mistake, and it won't ever be happening again. I thought we made that clear when I kicked you out of my house this morning.

I expect some type of argument, because, hello, he is Graham, but instead, a picture comes through of his neck that is covered in hickeys with a message.

Graham: If you say so, Davidson, but you and I both know that this is far from over.

This time, I do groan out loud, because what in the hell am I doing? I'm annoyed at myself, and at him.

I shove my phone back into my desk drawer after typing a message to Holland that I'll be making an emergency visit after work today. One, because I want to see my nephew, and two, because there is no way in hell I'm going to be able to keep this a secret from my best friend, and also because I need some accountability, since I obviously have a problem with only thinking about what my vagina wants.

Realistically, I know exactly the type of guy Graham is. I've known him for years, and I know his track record. There's a reason I don't date athletes, and there's an even better reason why I don't like Graham. So, him having a magic dick... doesn't change that.

Staying away from him is the only option. Period.

I spend the rest of the day researching cases for Rob, not giving myself the opportunity to think about Graham, or the hot, sweaty, ridiculously good sex we had last night, until I'm shutting my computer down and pulling my purse out at well past six to leave for the day.

I even put on my favorite true crime podcast on the ride to Holland and Reed's house because I'm avoiding thinking about last night and all of the things that Graham made me feel.

I'm truly the queen of avoidance, but it's for a good reason.

When I pull into Holland's driveway, I shut off the podcast and grab my bag then walk inside through the side door.

The second I walk in, I smell my mom's lasagna and almost panic that she's here, then I remember that Holland has been spending time with Ma, trying to learn her recipes. She's on this new "wifey" thing where she wants to cook every single night for Evan, and Reed.

I shudder. I am not made for this kind of life. I am so glad I get to be the cool aunt and that actual living, breathing humans don't have to depend on me.

"Holl, I'm here," I call from the mudroom, where I kick off my heels and hang my bag on the designated hooks.

Before I even make it to the kitchen, Evan comes barreling around the corner with a Nerf gun that's twice as big as him, wearing full tactical gear. An actual vest that reads SWAT, goggles, and a belt that houses hundreds of plastic bullets.

"Hands up Auntie Em or surrender to the United States of Uhmeri-cuh."

I laugh then quickly plaster on a concerned face, raising my hands. "What am I being accused of, sir?"

He thinks on it for a second, letting his gun lower slightly, then quickly raises it back up. "Because it's been five whole entire days since you came to visit me."

Only my nephew has the ability to soften me to a pile of mush with only a few words. He has me wrapped entirely around his finger.

"I'm sorry, buddy, I have been so busy with work. How about we go to the movies soon? Oh, or, what about the arcade?"

Evan grins, his eyes lighting up. "Okay. You don't have to surrender."

I laugh. "Thanks. Where's Aunt Holl and Uncle Reed?"

He shrugs. "I told Uncle Reed to hide and I kinda forgot about him when you got here."

"You know he hides in the same three places. Betcha he's in the closet in the bathroom."

"Oh yeah, I forgot about that one. Bye Auntie Em," he calls behind him as he takes off toward the stairs.

I follow behind him into the kitchen, where I find the sauce simmering on the stove, and the tell-tale sign of garlic knots in the oven and my mouth waters.

I've felt queasy all day after drinking so much, and I can't wait to eat.

"Holl?" I call, still searching for my best friend.

Seconds later, she appears, cheeks flushed, and her shirt on backwards.

I groan. I swear these two have sex like rabbits, and while I'm so unbelievably happy for my best friend and my favorite, okay only, brother, I still do not want to think about them having sex.

Gross.

"Em, hey, sorry I was just uh..." She turns red, stumbling over her words.

Reed walks in behind her, a grin on his lips. "She was doing laundry."

Nodding, she looks relieved. "Right, I was folding mountains of clothes."

It's actually sort of comical how embarrassed she gets when it comes to Reed, even after all these years. They've been married for years now, and it feels like forever, but that's probably because I've been subjected to this torture for so long.

"Mhm, is that what you two are calling it these days?"

This time Reed shrugs shamelessly. "Sorry, Em, but my wife is hot as fuck, and I can't help that I want to fu-"

He's cut off when Holland slaps her hand over his mouth, turning red once more. "You. Out. Or it'll be the last time we ever do laundry together."

Reed mumbles against her hand until she yelps. "Did you just lick me? Oh god, would you go find Evan?"

He laughs, dipping down to give her a way too hot kiss. These two are so in love it's sickening.

Sometimes when I see them, or any of our friends being so... domesticated, I think I want a stable, dependable relationship, and then something comes along and changes that way of thinking quickly.

Once he's gone, Holland looks at me with a lovesick smile and sighs. "Sorry."

"Don't apologize, Holl. I love seeing you happy. But what would make me happier is some of this lasagna. I'm hungover and starving."

She laughs, walking over to the stove and stirring the pot of sauce, then pulling it from the burner. "You Davidsons are all the same. Now tell me what's the emergency."

Sitting down at the bar across from the stove, I sink further into the barstool and then I scan the kitchen, to make sure Reed and Evan aren't both still hiding, and whisper it because I'll actually die if my brother hears, "I had sex with Graham."

"What?"

I say it louder, still avoiding her gaze. "I had sex with Graham."

She huffs. "I can't hear you when you're whispering from across the room, Emery."

"I had sex with Graham!" I all but scream. It echoes around the kitchen slightly, and I groan, dropping my head onto my arms.

"I'm pretty sure I just heard you say you had sex with Graham. Like as in the LEFT WING, aka manwhore of the century?" Holland screeches.

Oh god, this is actual torture.

"You heard right. Holland, I couldn't help it, my vagina has a brain of her own apparently. Ugh, my brain is completely jumbled right now."

She abandons the sauce and comes over to the bar, taking a seat next to me. "Oh Em. Are you okay?" Not even waiting for my response, she tugs me into her arms and gives me a tight hug.

That's my best friend. I could burn down the Eiffel Tower, and she'd still ask if I was okay. She's my late night, get-out-of-jail call, and she'd do so without judgment.

I nod. "I just... knew better. And I don't do... athletes. Ever."

Holland shakes her head with wide eyes. "I know, but what actually happened? I saw him follow you out, but I honestly didn't think you'd be.. I don't know, hooking up?"

"Ugh, I don't know. Last night we were drinking, and then somehow, we ended up at my house and had sex against the front door. The front door, Holl. Like I'm in college and not an actual adult with a law degree and a good head on my shoulders. Not that it's ever going to happen again."

She doesn't look convinced. "You do know that Graham has had the hots for you for practically ever?"

Uh, no I don't actually think that's true. She wasn't there that night, she didn't overhear what I did.

"No, he just has the hots for everyone with a vagina, Holland. Duh."

"Okay, true. Well, if you don't want it to happen again, then whatever, just pretend it never happened. I'm sure Graham is probably already on his next conquest. I love him, I do, but the guy has a new girl for every day of the week."

That statement shouldn't cause a knot to form in my stomach, since it's true, and I know it, but it does.

I don't actually want to think of Graham with another girl. Don't ask me why, because I couldn't even tell you.

"Good for him. Hopefully he keeps his mouth shut, and we'll just move on like it never happened."

She nods, reaching out and pulling me in for another hug. I sink into the embrace, feeling slightly better now that I've told my best friend and gotten her advice.

"I'm on your side, babe. Look, I've been there and done that. Don't beat yourself up. We all do things that are out of character, and it isn't necessarily a bad thing. Take it day by day. Be the bad bitch you always are."

She's right. We can pretend it never happened and move on. Easy peasy. He knows I don't have any interest in a relationship, so there's no issue here.

It's not like it'll ever happen again.

A one and done. Okay... a few times and done. Fine.

Done, all the same.

I am completely and utterly *done* with Graham Adams and his voodoo magic dick.

GRAHAM

SIX

ME: **You gonna keep eye fucking me or do you want to let everyone know I made you come?**

Smirking, I press send and glance directly across the table, taunting Emery with my eyes. She's pretending not to stare my way, but every time I sneak a glance at her, those blue eyes are staring right back. The best thing about this "thing" we've got going on? How much she hates me but loves what I do to her body.

If she had it her way, she'd been fine never seeing me again after the first night, but seeing as how we run in the same circle, there's no way she can avoid me for that long and thank fuck for that because now that I've had a taste of Emery Davidson, she's consuming every thought I have.

I probably shouldn't be thinking about her pussy while we're at her brother's house, sitting at the dinner table, surrounded by our friends, but here we are. It's a fantastic pussy. Tight like my favorite pair of gloves, warm and snug whenever I slide insi-

"Adams."

My eyes dart to Briggs, who's holding a piece of pizza up with his eyebrow raised in question.

"What?"

"I've been calling your name for five minutes. You want pepperoni or meat lovers."

Shrugging, I say, "Don't care."

He tosses a slice on a plate and passes it my way, all while I sneak another peek at Emery, who's now reading something on her phone. Undoubtedly, the message I sent her, just to see the reaction I'd get.

There's nothing more I love then seeing just how far I can push her until she loses it, and, hopefully, it will somehow lead to her riding my cock.

My grin widens when I see her grind her teeth together and look up at me through her thick lashes, shooting daggers across the table. Mission accomplished.

I sit back, taking a bite out of the pizza, and wink at her, then focus back on the conversation, before someone around us *does* realize what's happening. As much as I want Emery to scream my name from the rooftops, what I don't want is our friends to find out what's going on. I don't want shit to be weird; I don't want Reed to shove my balls in a glass jar and put it on a shelf in his trophy room. I don't want anything to change.

I like the dynamic of our friendships.

It made working together as a team work seamlessly, flawlessly since we are all so close and hockey is my life.

The easiest choice I ever made was deciding to be a professional hockey player. It was a no brainer for me. I grew up on the ice with a stick and a puck. When I wasn't in school or working on the farm, I was on the ice. Pushing my body and my mind to the limits, working overtime to be better. Faster.

Stronger. But, I was all my mama and Allie had, and being the man of the house was my responsibility.

When I was drafted, fresh out of college, it was a dream come true, but to this day, I still feel guilty about leaving mama and Allie to come to a new city to pursue my dreams. And that same nagging guilt always resurfaces when I score a goal or celebrate a good pass.

Leaving my family behind was the hard part of playing hockey. Having to move to a new city, where I knew no one, with a bank account that had more zeroes then I'd ever seen in my life, and how different life was in the blink of an eye. One second, I was mucking a stall and studying for a farming management degree, and the next, I was in a stadium where thousands of people were chanting my name like I was a god.

As much as I loved every aspect of being a pro player, I was lonely. Until Reed took me under his wing and the guys became my found family.

They're the only ones I've got, and I'll never do anything to jeopardize what I have with them.

Emery Davidson included.

So, if she wants me to chase her. Fuck it, I'll chase her around the entire city, but I'm going to make sure no one knows about it, and I happen to know that would suit her just fine.

I knew my message would make her mad, and now's time for the second part of my plan. She can ignore my texts all week, if that makes her feel better, but sitting face to face is a completely different thing.

Standing, I toss the pizza crust onto the plate in front of me and head to the upstairs bathroom, taking the stairs two at a time. I slip inside and shut the door behind me, then lean against the vanity and wait.

Not to sound cocky but... I can tell she wants this just as badly as I do.

A few seconds later, the door opens and Emery appears, her blue eyes blazing. She shuts the door behind her and stalks toward me. Her dark hair billowing behind her with each step.

"Really Graham?"

I smirk. "What? Can't get enough of me?"

She reaches out with her tiny, albeit powerful, fist and punches me in the shoulder, causing me to wince.

I rub the spot tenderly. "What the *fuck* was that for?"

"Because your ego literally knows no bounds, and because that was totally inappropriate. Reed was sitting right next to me!"

Okay, true. But I couldn't help myself. Something tells me that agreeing with her isn't going to help the situation.

"I told you it's done between us. Didn't you get that when I didn't respond to your ridiculously gross text messages?'

Shrugging, I push off the vanity, stepping closer to her. Her sweet, cinnamon scent fills my nostrils and never in my life have I fucking craved Red Hots.

You know, the little cinnamon candies that burn the fuck out of your tongue, yet you still eat them like an insane person. That's what Emery is, not even five feet tall, but she's red hot, from the top of her head to the tips of her toes. Especially when she's mad. It's the hottest taste of cinnamon I've ever had.

I watch as she swallows, stepping back slightly until she is pressed against the back of the door. Placing my hand on the side of her head, I dip lower, inhaling.

"Did you just... sniff me?" She screeches.

I nod. "You smell so goddamn good; it's driving me insane."

Her hands float to my chest and she pushes with little effort.

While Emery is in denial about what's really happening here, I, on the other hand, am fully aware of how badly I want her: beneath me, above me, in front of me while I fuck her from behind.

The truth is, the taste I had of Emery was never going to be enough. I've wanted it every damn day since, and I'm not going to stop until she lets me have her without inhibition. Did I know better than to sleep with my best friend's sister? Did I know how complicated shit would be once I did?

Yep, but only if anyone found out, and right now, with her pressed against the door, chest heaving, pupils dilated and my cock straining against the zipper of my jeans, none of it matters.

I'll deal with the consequences later.

"I know you're not used to women actually telling you no, but this thing," she gestures between us, "is over. Done. I'm bored, and I have no interest in continuing it."

"Prove it."

For a moment, she looks surprised, like she didn't actually expect me to call her on her bullshit.

"W-w-what?" she sputters.

"I said... prove it. You keep saying you don't want me, and that it's done... so prove it. Walk away. No more orgasms, and no more hookups."

While I whisper the words, I drag my hand to the waistband of her shorts, rubbing my thumb along the exposed skin of her crop top. She looks up at me through thick lashes, sucking her bottom lip into her mouth whenever I dip below the button of her shorts to the string of her underwear and slide my finger beneath it.

"I hate you," she says simply, even though the heavy-lidded look she gives me says otherwise.

"There's a thin line between lust and hate, Emery. How about you stop thinking for five seconds and let me make you come on my face before someone downstairs realizes we're gone."

"God, you're *foul*. Your mouth."

Yet, here we fucking are. She happens to love this mouth, especially whenever it's sucking on her clit, and I know that when I slide my fingers just a *liiiiitle* bit farther into her panties, I'll find her already wet for me. This cat and mouse game we play turns her on just as much as it does me. So she can pretend all she wants, but I'm not buying a single second of it.

I don't answer her; instead, I drop to my knees in front of her, our eyes locked as I undo the button of her shorts and tug on the bottoms, pulling them down her hips. Today she's got on a bright pink, lace thong that makes my mouth water. The lace covering her pussy is damp, and I lightly rub my nose along the fabric while she hisses.

Teasing her further, I swipe along the damp fabric with my tongue, before nipping at her clit.

"Should I stop?" I ask her, her lust filled dilated eyes searing into mine.

"Stop and you die," she mutters, threading her hands in my hair, grasping onto the ends for dear life when I pull the tiny triangle aside and take a long, slow swipe of my tongue along her pussy. When my lips close around her clit, the soft sigh-like mewl that leaves her mouth almost gets us caught.

"Quiet Emery," I mumble against her pussy as I begin to devour her. I suck her clit into my mouth, eating her like the starved man I am. When she lets out another moan, I pull her leg from my shoulder and lay her down on the floor, then shove two fingers inside her mouth and demand her to "suck."

She starts to argue, but I raise my eyebrow, telling her to only defy me... if she wants me to be done eating her pussy. She rolls her eyes, but she also opens her mouth, allowing my fingers to slide against her velvet tongue.

"Suck." I say once more.

This time, there's no arguing, she simply sucks my fingers into her mouth, flattening her tongue against the pads of my fingers. I press farther into her mouth until my fingers are sliding down her throat. She gags slightly, and I smirk.

"Should be my cock, but I know you're scared to actually make this a "thing"."

She raises her eyebrows in defiance.

I shrug.

Her hands pull my fingers free and she sits up on her elbows. "Actually, I'm not afraid of this," she gestures between us, "in the slightest, but I, on the other hand, don't hang on after a one-night stand, unlike you."

I roll my eyes then rub my thumb against her clit, watching as her head drops back and her eyes close. Her lips part, and her body relaxes.

"You can say it all fucking day, Davidson, but the truth is, I fucked you like no one else ever has, and you know it. Deep down, under all of that attitude and sass. That's why you fucked me the first time, and that's why I'm on my knees in front of you with your pussy still on my tongue..."

Her blue eyes meet mine again, and she doesn't protest. Seconds pass, as I continue to rub her clit, but she shoves my hand and rises to her knees, then pushes against my chest, hard, until I'm flat on my ass, my back pressed against the door.

She crawls forward on her hands and knees, and I take a

mental picture at how fucking hot she looks. Her lips swollen and bruised from my kiss, her eyes wide with both desire and defiance, a fire that I love to stoke.

"You talk a lot of shit, Adams," she whispers as she reaches out and deftly flicks the button of my jeans open, then slowly, so fucking slow, drags my zipper downward.

"Gotta, to keep up with that mouth." I smirk, reaching out to drag my thumb along her plump bottom lip.

I might talk a lot of shit, but that was the truth. She wants me, just as badly as I want her, and at the end of the day, if she needs to pretend she doesn't want me, then so be it. Whatever helps her sleep at night. I know better.

Eventually, she's going to have to be honest with herself.

Her hands yank my briefs down my hips until my cock springs free. I'm hard as fuck, and when she wraps her tiny hand around my head and squeezes, spreading the drop of precum that's beading at the slit, I suck in a hiss.

"Ah, better be quiet, Adams." She smirks cheekily, and then leans down, making a perfect O with those plump lips around my cock.

My soul leaves my fucking body. I bring my hand up to her hair, lacing my fingers into the hair at her nape and tugging gently as she looks up at me while she hollows her cheeks and sucks.

"Fuuuuuuck." I groan, guiding her head up and down on my cock, farther and farther until the head presses against the back of her throat. Gagging slightly, she doesn't pause, she only opens her mouth wider, taking all of me until the short, landscaped hair on my groin is against her nose as she deep throats me.

"Jesus Christ, marry me. Right the fuck now," I whisper, half joking, half not. The red-lipped vixen with my cock in her mouth has me losing my fucking mind. Okay I'm not being serious, but I am seeing stars.

My words make her pause and she promptly takes my dick out of her mouth, wiping away the spit from her chin.

"Way to ruin the moment."

"I was joking," I protest.

Before I can pull her back to me, there's a loud knock at the door that has it vibrating against my back. A stark reminder to the fact that we just did this shit in one of her brother's bathrooms.

We're both losing our fucking mind.

Lust does that to you.

Her eyes widen, and she scrambles to her feet, trying to fix her clothes. "Uh, someone's in here, one second."

"I know, I have to pee! Briggs is in the other bathroom. Hurry!" Holland's voice comes from the other side of the door.

I almost sigh in relief.

"Okay!" Emery's voice is barely a squeak, and I have to bite my lip not to laugh. It's rare to see Emery... nervous, but she's shitting her pants right now.

She narrows her eyes at me as Holland's footsteps retreat. "You're making me crazy. This is *not* happening again."

"Kay."

I don't even bother to argue with her because we both know that shit's a lie. I just tuck myself back in my pants, as much as I'd rather fucking not, then reach out and fix the smeared lipstick on the corner of her lip.

"See you soon, *babe.*"

I grin, then walk out the door, for once leaving *Emery Davidson* speechless.

EMERY

SEVEN

SINCE THAT DAY at Holland and Reed's house, I've been avoiding Graham. Well, avoiding being alone with him. Since that's when I apparently become a weak-ass bitch, nothing like myself, and end up below or above him.

He's been relentless, texting me about his day and how he misses being between my legs. Making it nearly impossible to go back to how it was before. Before G-day is what we'll call it. It's been two months since we've been alone, but tonight, I can't avoid him any longer. I've been throwing myself into work, doing anything and everything not to think about him since I'm desperately trying to purge him from my body and mind.

It's Liam and Juliet's anniversary party, and if I don't show up, Juliet will be heartbroken. So, that means that I'll have to spend at least a few hours in the same room as him, and my willpower is a fickle bitch when he's involved.

I'm trying. I haven't responded to his texts, even when he sent me a picture from the shower that was NSFW, featuring so many abs I lost count, along with that oblique muscle that I want to run my tongue along. I'm a reformed addict, and the first step is to leave the thing you're addicted to alone.

I've been sitting in my car for the past fifteen minutes, pep-talking myself and trying to devise a game plan that keeps me far, far away. Pulling my visor down, I check my lip gloss once more in the mirror, grab my clutch from the passenger seat, then get out.

While I knew that I would be staying away from Graham, that didn't mean that I couldn't make his mouth water from across the room tonight. The little black dress I'm wearing is cut low, yet still classy, and hugs each dip and curve of my body like it was made for me. It took an entire day of trying on at least fifty different dresses, but I finally found the perfect dress and I have no doubt the moment he lays eyes on me, he's going to lose it.

I know what he likes, and this... this dress was made to be devoured by him. Paired with a pair of my tallest Louboutins, which make my legs look fucking amazing, and I'm wearing the brightest red lipstick I have.

I walk to the front, and through the doors of the building that they've rented for tonight and walk inside. The entire building is decked out in tasteful gold and blush, and it looks like another wedding.

Leave it to Liam to go all out for his wife. My eyes canvas the room, and I find the happy couple dancing to the slow, reverbed beat in the center of the room, along with Briggs and Maddison, and their daughter. Across the room, I see Reed and Holland, laughing at whatever Hudson is saying.

"Looking for me?" A low, velvet voice purrs in my ear, and I don't need to even turn to know who the voice belongs to.

"And why would I be doing that?"

Hot breath fans out against the back of my neck, causing

me to shiver. "I hope you know that I'm going to tear that dress off of you the second I get you alone, Davidson. So goddamn hot. You're lucky we're surrounded by people or I'd already have it on the floor."

His words hold promise, but I'm saying strong. I step forward and turn around, crossing my arms over my chest. "I told you we're done, Graham, have fun tonight though."

Spinning on my heel, I leave him standing there and march toward Reed and Holland. My restraint is shaky at best, and right now, I have to put distance between us.

"Hey sis," Reed says, pulling me in for a hug. He's in a tux with a red tie that matches the same hue of Holland's deep red dress. It looks amazing on her.

"Hey guys." I say, taking a flute of champagne as the waiter passes by with a tray. Tonight, I'm going to need all the liquid courage I can get.

"You look so hot bitch!" Holland squeals, taking my hand.

"Uh, says you... you look like a movie star," I tell her, twisting my hand around one of her curls.

"Gonna go grab me a beer, babe, you want anything?" Reed asks her.

She shakes her head no, offering a small smile. "Thank you."

Once he's gone, she leans closer. "So, I have to tell you something."

"Okay, spill." Bringing the flute to my lips, I drain the last of the champagne in one long sip and set it on the table next to her.

"I'm pregnant."

I all but swallow my tongue. "What?"

Her eyes light up and she nods. "I just found out before we got here. I'm having a *baby*, Em."

Tears well in my eyes and I pull her to me, giving her a hug. When I pull back, the tears in my eyes match her own. "Oh God, Holl, I'm so happy for you and Reed. You both deserve this so much. Evan is going to be such a great big brother!"

She lets out a watery laugh. "We told him tonight before we left him with the sitter. He said that he's going to give one of his toys to the new baby, and I cried. I can't stop crying!" She reaches up and dries the tears from her eyes and shakes her head.

My heart squeezes.

Seeing my brother and my best friend become parents to Evan was one of the best experiences of my life, and now I get to see Holl pregnant.

"I can't believe I get to be an aunt again!" I screech.

"I can't believe I'm actually pregnant, I mean... we've kind of been trying for a while and I was starting to get worried, and then I took a test and it was positive."

I nod. "It happens like that sometimes. How far along do you think you are?"

"I think eight weeks, but I'll find out at my appointment next week."

Reed strolls back up as Holland and I hug again, with a proud smirk. "Guess she told you the news?"

"Yes. Congratulations. I'm so happy for you both."

"Who knew we'd be here all those years ago, huh?" he says, sipping his beer. "Love happens unexpectedly."

Nodding, I think about Graham, but then quickly push the thought away. Graham Adams and love should never be associated together, not at any point.

I lift my gaze to scan the room and find him across the dance floor, laughing with his coach and coach's wife, and then his eyes lock with mine. It's almost as if there's an invisible string that's somehow connecting us across the room. A pull. Like magnets gravitating toward one another, but never close enough to connect.

"Em?"

I tear my eyes from his, and look back at Reed, who's calling my name.

"Yeah, sorry, what?"

He laughs. "I wanna introduce you to Coach Williamson's son. He's at Johnson & Skelter. First-year too."

"Oh sure."

We walk over to the same group of guys that Graham is talking to, and Reed makes introductions. I say a polite hello and do a decent job at keeping my gaze off Graham.

"Ross, this is Emery, my sister. She just got licensed and is a first-year at Johsnon and Montgomery. Wanted to make the introduction."

Is Reed trying to play... matchmaker? What in the hell is happening right now?

I smile politely. "Hi, I'm Emery, but everyone calls me Em."

Ross isn't unattractive, not by any means. He's the exact type of guy I go for. Tall, dark hair, clean cut, strong jaw. Tom Ford taste. Good head on his shoulders, but the classic can't commit type. Suits me perfectly fine.

He steps a bit away from the group and gestures for me to join him. "I know this is a bit forward, but you're gorgeous."

I laugh. "Thanks."

Hearing a scoff, I turn toward Graham, who's standing next to Reed pretending to partake in small talk. I narrow my eyes at him then bring my attention back to Ross and smile sweetly.

"So how are you liking being an associate? Were you with them before you passed the bar?"

89

"Yeah, I've been interning since I was in law school. It's great, I've just taken on a really great case and I'm excited to get to work."

He nods, a wide smile on his too perfect teeth. "That's great. We should get dinner sometime and discuss work. And other things."

"Oh sure. My schedule is pretty packed right now though."

"Well, I'll get your number before I leave. How about a dance?"

God this is awkward as hell. Getting asked out in front of the man my vagina is apparently obsessed with is beyond uncomfortable.

"Uh, sure."

He offers me his hand, and I follow him out onto the dance floor. Another slow, seductive melody plays through the speaker, and when he places his hand on the small of my back and pulls me forward, I swallow thickly.

We move back and forth to the music, all while making small talk, until a shadow hovers over us. When I look up, I see Graham standing there, looking more pissed than I've ever seen him with his jaw steeled.

"Can I cut in?"

Ross looks from him to me then back at him. "Well, man, we're dancing so gonna have to say no."

Graham laughs without an ounce of humor. "Good thing I wasn't really asking."

My eyes widen. This is his coach's son. I see this situation deteriorating, *quickly*.

"What's your problem, Adams?" Ross turns toward Graham. His stance rigid, he grits his teeth together and waits for Graham's response. This entire situation is turning me off, of Ross especially.

He shrugs. "I'm saying you should probably take your hands off of her, before I take them off for you."

Oh my god. This is not actually happening right now.

"She your girl?" Ross stares at Graham, who grits his teeth and steps closer. His posture is rigid, and he looks like he's going to beat the shit out of this guy. "Doesn't matter, Ross. Take your fucking hands off of her."

This time I stop, letting go of Ross and stepping between them, because they're starting to cause a scene that none of us want.

"Hey, stop. Graham stop," I say, placing my hands on his chest.

Ross scoffs, shaking his head. "Ah, I must've missed the memo. Good luck with *that* Emery." He walks away, leaving Graham and me alone.

"What the fuck was that?" I seethe through clenched teeth. "You should have just pulled your dick out and pissed all over me, Graham. I am not anyone's property and sure as hell *not* yours."

I stalk away, leaving him alone on the dance floor, and bust through the exit doors. There's fire in my veins right now; I'm beyond livid. He has no right to act like this.

The cool air hits my cheeks as I suck in a deep, full breath. Seconds later, the door busts open, and Graham stalks toward me. Even angry, I can't help but notice how handsome he looks in his suit. The cut fits his body perfectly, showcasing his broad, thick shoulders.

He never pauses, never hesitates, he grabs my face in his hands and slams his lips on mine, drinking me in. I never realized how tense; how tight my body was until I sank into his embrace. I feel his kiss down to the tips of my toes. He cradles my jaw in his hands and angles his head to the side to deepen our kiss, sucking my tongue and making me whimper against his mouth.

It's enough to almost make me forget why I was angry in the first place.

Almost.

Not quite.

I rip my lips from his and step back, panting. "Do not try to control this situation by kissing me."

He shakes his head, running a hand roughly through his dirty blonde hair. "Tha- That's not what I was doing Emery."

I scoff and roll my eyes, stepping farther away; keeping space between us is my only defense. My only way to keep him at arm's length, both literally and figuratively. "Could've fooled me."

"Listen, I lost my head okay. I'm sorry. Okay? I'm fucking sorry. It made me... I- don't fucking know... *insane* to see him touch you. Out of my damn mind."

"Graham, *this* is insane." I throw my hands up in exasperation. This thing that was never supposed to happen is slowly turning into something entirely different. Dropping my head in my hands, I groan. I've been trying to get him off my mind for months, and this just makes everything worse. It seems like every time I see him, we're falling right back into a pattern.

A situation.

Something out of my control.

Something I don't want and never will.

"Em, c'mere, please," he says, pulling my hands away and swiping at my bottom lip. The gesture is gentle and intimate, and I don't quite know how to feel about this. Any of this.

It's too much.

I step back. "Graham, I'm not doing this. Look, I said from the start that I wasn't interested in pursuing... frenemies-with-benefits. I meant it. I don't want a relationship; I don't want the white picket fence and the kids. The serious, committed relationship. And tonight? How you just acted... it's just too much. I'm not yours, I'm not your property. You have no right, no claim over anyone touching me or asking me out." I watch as the muscle in his jaw ticks as he grinds his teeth at my words, but it's not like I haven't been saying this from the start.

He's the one who won't listen. Tonight proved that things are messy, and complicated and that's the opposite of what I want.

Mind-blowing sex or not.

I knew better than to let this happen. I did. I knew better, and I didn't listen to my head. I thought it would be just sex, and tonight proved that it's beyond that.

"Eme-"

Holding my hand up to stop him, I raise my chin higher. This is not who I am. I know exactly the person I am and what I want out of life. I'm fine with casual, no strings, but not a jealous hookup. "How you acted tonight, like a jealous boyfriend? No, I'm done with this. Please don't call me again. Tell my brother and Holland I wasn't feeling well and I left. I think I've made it clear that this isn't what I want."

Why do all of this after saying he didn't want me, and that he wasn't interested. What happened to him being the hookup guy? Why has he suddenly flipped the script?

Now, more than ever, I'm confused.

I don't give him a chance to respond; I turn on my heels and walk away. Clean break. That's what we need. Even if it sucks to do it, I can't and won't lose myself in Graham.

GRAHAM

EIGHT

I'M PRETTY SURE the last place I should be is standing on Emery's doorstep. Actually, I know I shouldn't be here. I should be at the gym, or the rink, or hell, doing anything but standing here. There are more than enough reasons not to be here; yet, here I am, holding a paper bag of my mama's chicken noodle soup and so many different cold medicines that the person checking me out at the pharmacy probably thought I was starting a meth lab.

When Emery sees me, she'll probably throw one of those pointy heels that I love so much right at my head, praying that it takes me out.

Red hot. And I don't even give a shit, what I do give a shit about is knowing Em's okay.

It's been two weeks since I've seen her, and two weeks since she told me to shove it up my ass after how I acted at the anniversary party. Which, I do feel like shit about, but I felt even fucking worse seeing that prick's hands on her. When Reed mentioned that she was sick, I couldn't stand by and do nothing.

I use the sleek black knocker on the door and wait. Thirty seconds go by and nothing, so I knock again. I'm about to pull my phone out and call when the door swings open and Emery appears.

Oh fuck.

Her eyes are red-rimmed and puffy and her nose looks like fucking Rudolph, and she's wearing at least seven layers of clothes on under the blanket draped on her shoulders.

She groans, dropping her head against the side of the door, leaning on it for support. "Please tell me I'm hallucinating, and you aren't actually standing here."

I laugh. "Nice to see you too, babe. Brought you something."

Her eyes drift down to the paper bag in my right hand, and her eyes light up slightly. "Is it something to put me out of my misery?"

"Nope, something better. You gonna let me in?"

For a second, she pauses, and I think she might say no, which she probably should but then she straightens and opens the door wider for me to enter. If I didn't know how sick she was by her appearance, her house would be a dead giveaway.

It's a fucking wreck, and while wild Emery Davidson is a spitfire and as wild as they come, messy she is not.

"Damn," I mutter, taking in the living room and kitchen. There's junk everywhere, half-empty water bottles and soup cans littering the counter.

Instead of responding, she breaks out in a coughing fit that has me dumping the stuff in my arms onto the counter and rushing to her. She doubles over, clutching her chest as she hacks, and when I reach out to put my arm around her, she sinks into my touch.

"Goddamn it, Emery, have you been to the doctor?"

She shakes her head then groans, still clutching her chest. "No, I hate doctors."

This woman. Stubborn as fuck.

"You sound like you're dying. Go sit down at least." I guide her to the couch and she plops down onto the plush white of her sectional, curling into the blanket around her shoulders. "Are you cold?"

She nods slightly. "I can't get warm."

"That's because I'm sure you have the flu. Do you have a thermometer?"

"I'm fine, Graham, you don't have to be here. Didn't we say this was over?"

Even though she's not fine and another coughing fit hits her just as she says it. If I left right now, I'd feel like an asshole. When Reed told me she was sick, in passing, and that she sounded like shit over the phone, I knew my Ma's soup would make everything better. It always did for me when I was growing up, and honestly? What happened at the party is the last thing I'm worried about. Right now, at least. Because I wasn't going to let her walk away so easily. Nah, not when I can feel what's happening between us. I've never been one to give up when it came to something I wanted, and what I want is Emery.

"Look, I get that we're done with the benefits part of this, but you're sick as hell, Em. Can't we at least be friends? Let me take care of you. Plus, I brought my mama's famous chicken noodle soup. Now where's the thermometer?" I raise my eyebrow.

"Wait, doesn't your family live in like Idaho or something, how did you even the get soup here?"

"Tennessee. And because I made it."

With that, she sits up slightly, her eyes wide. "You... made me chicken noodle soup? *Homemade?*" Disbelief drips from her words.

I shrug. "It's no big deal."

"Oh god," she groans, flopping back down, "I was right. You are too good to be true. This feels relationship-y. Your mom's homemade chicken noodle soup? No. I can't Adams, sorry. I'm okay. Leave me to die alone. Seriously, out."

Her dramatics make me grin. A girl after my own heart. I've been called dramatic a few times in my life.

"Don't make it a big deal. I'm going to look in the medicine cabinet for the thermometer."

"Fine," she grumbles, snuggling into the blanket. I'm almost to the door of her bathroom when I hear her speak.

"Graham?"

"Yeah?" I look back at her.

"I still hate you."

"Still don't care, babe."

———

After a few minutes of searching for the thermometer, I finally find one and take her temperature, which comes back at almost a hundred and three, cementing the fact that she probably does have the flu... or something worse. I read the labels of all of the medicines I got at the pharmacy and give her one with a pain reliever.

With her fever being so high, it's no surprise that she's fast asleep before I can even take the soup out of the bag, so instead, I throw away some of the bottles and takeout containers.

I feel domesticated as fuck right now, and I know better than to ever voice it to her, but fuck... I like being here with Emery.

I'm liking it far too much to be doing this with a woman I can't have. I know her and her defenses. Emery puts up a wall, but everything about her makes me want to tear it down just to get to her.

Once I'm done in the kitchen, I warm up the soup and fix her a bowl, then grab her a bottle of water and another dose of medicine. Setting it down, I pull the blankets back from her face and for a moment... just a single moment, my eyes study her face, drinking her in.

Even sick as a dog, Emery Davidson is breathtaking. She has a way of making me trip over my feet while I'm standing still.

"Em," I whisper, pushing a loose piece of hair from her damp forehead. The fever's broke, so the medicine must be working.

She lets out a groggy groan, then cracks open an eye. "Graham?"

I grin. "The one and only."

Shakily, she pulls herself into a sitting position and looks around the room. "What happened? Oh god, I feel like I got run over with a Zamboni. Everything. Hurts."

She falls back to the couch and groans.

"That's it. Get up, you're going to the doctor. You need fluid. Antibiotics. UP."

The look she gives me is one that says I should probably duck and cover my nuts, but instead, she shakily sits up and crosses her arms over her chest.

"Just know I'm only agreeing because I am way too hot to die. I haven't even been to Paris yet. I've always wanted to go to Paris, and I can't die before I get there."

My lips tug into a grin as I lean down and help her up, looping my arm around her waist and lifting her easily.

"Gonna throw on a hoodie and put on real shoes." Glancing down at her slippers, she frowns. "Although I think my bunny slippers are chic, I don't think the doctor will agree."

This girl is fucking even more hilarious when she's doped up on cold medicine.

"I'll wait here for you," I say, leaning against the frame of her door. My gaze never leaves her while she throws on an old Avalanche hoodie and trades the slippers for a pair of Converse. When she walks back through the door, her cheeks are flushed red and the bags under her eyes seem to have turned even darker.

"Let's go, you look terrible."

Her eyes roll. "Thanks. I feel like a corpse."

"You're sick, Em. We'll get you to the doctor and then you'll be back to your sassy self in no time."

"Lucky you."

I help her into my SUV, and after a quick drive, we arrive at her doctor. Thank fuck they were able to squeeze her in; I'm sure it had everything to do with the fact that she looks and sounds like death.

It took me at least five minutes to convince her to let me come inside with her to the doctor. And another thirty to get her there, out of the car and into the waiting room. Friends do things like this, or at least that was my argument. I get it, she's got this aversion to commitment, and she's ready to dart at the first sign of feelings, but I'm not leaving her alone when she's this sick. She can think what she wants, but I'm a good guy, and I wasn't about to be an asshole and leave her by herself.

Fun fact. I hate going to the doctor alone. A grown ass man who is terrified of doctors, and even more afraid of needles. Not that I was going to let Emery know that. Matter of fact, she forbid me from even talking when the doctor entered the room, so I'm a church mouse as I watch the nurse takes her vitals, and asks her a series of questions.

"After I swab you for the flu, and for mono, I'm going to bring back a cup for you to do a pregnancy test and then the doctor will be in to see you, Emery," a short, busty redheaded nurse says kindly, before pulling out a long as fuck Q-tip and promptly shoving it up Emery's nose all the way to her goddamn brain, then says a quick goodbye and exits the room.

"Jesus, that was an actual torture device. A pregnancy test?" I say, eyebrows raised.

She nods, sniffling. "Some medications can't be given to pregnant women, so they do a test each time before prescribing them."

"Hm."

A minute later, the nurse returns with a clear plastic cup; Emery follows her out of the door then returns soon after empty-handed.

"It hurts to even walk to the bathroom." She moans, hoisting herself back up on the table and lying back against the white tissue paper covering the table.

"They'll get you some medicine, and then when we get home, I'll heat the soup up for you again."

Sitting up on her elbows, she looks at me, her eyes slightly narrowed. "Why are you being so... sweet?"

"As opposed to being an asshole?" I shrug. "Not who I am. You said you're done with whatever we had going on, okay. I respect you and your decisions. You think I'd be a piece of shit to you because you decided to stop sleeping with me?"

She shakes her head then pulls her lip between her teeth before she answers, "I just... I don't know, most guys just don't take things like that well."

Before I can answer, the door opens and an older man, with

black hair that's peppered with gray, walks into the room, wearing a long white lab coat. The name tag on his coat says, "Dr. Montgomery."

"Hi Emery." He smiles, and then nods at me and extends his hand. "Hi, I'm Dr. Montgomery."

Sitting down on the round rolling stool across from Em, he looks at his clipboard and flips a few pages before glancing up through his glasses.

"Alright Emery, it looks like your flu test did come back as positive for influenza type A as well as strep throat, so that's probably what has you feeling so crummy. I'm going to take a quick look at your ears and throat, and have you breathe for me, so I can check your lungs.

"Thank you so much."

He checks her over fully then takes a seat back on the stool. "Yeah, your throat's pretty red, so we need to get you on some antibiotics. Although the antibiotics won't help the flu, since it's viral, it will clear up the strep throat. I'm going to prescribe a pretty mild antibiotic, so it doesn't hurt the baby." He smiles.

I would've sworn he just said baby, but I know I heard wrong.

"Baby?" Emery looks completely confused; her brow furrowed. "I think you have the wrong chart. No baby here." Laughing, she looks at me then back at him.

Dr. Montgomery lifts a paper on his clipboard and scans the sheet then shakes his head. "No, right here it shows that the administered pregnancy test came back positive. You're pregnant, Emery."

Pretty sure the floor just opened up and swallowed me fucking whole.

Pregnant?

THE SCORECARD

My gaze darts to Emery, who looks as pale as the sheet she's sitting on. What the hell is happening right now?

"That's im- impossible." She stutters over her words, obviously upset. "I'm on birth control, I don't- what?"

The Dr. Montgomery reaches out for her hand. "I didn't realize you were unaware, Emery. I'm sorry. This is your first pregnancy, so I know it can be scary and overwhelming. There is support for both you and your husband."

"He's not my husband! We just... we were hooking up." She screeches, yanking her hand free and covering her face. I hear a sniffle and realize she's fucking crying.

Fuck, this is the last thing I ever expected to find out when bringing her to the doctor for the flu. I mean... we were reckless. So caught up in the moment, but fuck, I thought she was on birth control? I thought we were okay. That's why we haven't used a condom, because I thought she was covered.

"Birth control isn't one hundred percent foolproof. There is always room for it to fail. It's nothing that you've done wrong or incorrectly. There's a failure rate for all medication," he says.

Emery shakes her head. "No. This can't be happening. I have the flu. I came here to get antibiotics... not be pregnant. I don't want- I didn't plan on ever having children."

The words cause my stomach to plummet. I just found out I'm going to be a dad.

I'm going to have my very own Olive.

Shock vibrates through my body. I don't know what to say or even to think right now.

"There are options, Emery. The first thing I would recommend is making an appointment with your gynecologist to discuss the options."

Options? What options? Not keeping our baby? My

105

stomach actually hurts at the thought. Now, I'm fucking nervous. Especially because Em is so upset.

She nods, swiping away tears and sucking in a breath. "Thank you."

Nodding, he gives her a sympathetic smile. "I'll get that prescription called into your pharmacy. If you need anything, please let me know. Make sure to drink plenty of fluids and get some rest. Feel better." He walks out the door, leaving us alone in silence.

The news sits heavy between us, hanging in the air.

"I- I.. I can't believe I'm *pregnant*." She sobs. "How did I not know? The s-s-hot makes me not have a period, but I mean, aren't there other symptoms? Nothing feels different. I've been tired, b-but-t I've been working so hard on this case, I didn't even notice. Oh... God. How could I not know?"

Fat tears stream down her face as she covers her mouth to stifle a sob.

I can't take the distance any longer, so I stand from the chair and walk over to her, placing my arms around her, holding her against my chest as her shoulders shake.

"It's going to be okay, Em," I tell her, even though I'm not so sure myself right now. I'm still in shock that I'm going to be a *father. A dad*. To a tiny little human who will look just like their mama, if they're lucky.

She shakes in my arms as she sobs against my chest. I can feel her tears soak through the material of my t-shirt, as I tighten my arms around her.

"How can you say that? How is it going to be okay? There is going to be someone who depends on us, Graham. Who we're responsible for. Who will rely on us to *live*. Everything will change, our entire lives will be different." She's rambling at this point, but I don't stop her. I share the same nerves she does, but another part of me... is excited. I fucking love kids. Unlike Emery, one day I do want the picket fence, the kids in the backyard chasing the dog, a big house with white shutters.

Just like how I grew up. In a happy, loving home.

Maybe that's happening sooner rather than later...

"... And I- I mean, I love wine. I can't drink wine all the time when I'm a mom. Oh god, I'm going to be fat and have cankles, and my tits. My tits," she sobs harder, "Maddison told me her boobs sag to her feet. To her feet, Graham! I have great tits, amazing ones really."

"They are amazing, truly. Perfection."

She pulls back and looks at me, covered in tears and snot, and still cute as fucking ever. "I will not lose my tits."

"You won't," I assure her.

"I'm scared."

Her voice is barely a whisper.

"Me too." I admit. "But, you'd be an amazing mother, Emery Davidson. I know it."

Freezing in my arms, she untangles herself. "Can you take me home? I just... I need medicine and time to process this. I can't make big decisions right now."

I nod. "Of course."

Reluctantly, I let her go and help her down from the table. I don't think we're any better off than when we got here, only now, we're leaving with some medicine and news that will change both our lives forever.

I don't know what the future will bring, and if I'm honest, I'm scared as fuck.

I've always wanted to be a father, and as nervous as I am about what is going to come, I'm hopeful that, even though she's presented with choices, she'll decide that having my baby is the one she wants.

EMERY

NINE

WHILE MOST OF THE TIME, I'm a strong, independent woman who has her shit together... this week has *rocked* my world. Titled it on its axis and made me question everything I thought I knew about what I wanted out of life.

You see, I've always had a plan. A steady, stable, strategic plan of how I expected my life to go.

And a baby was never part of that plan.

Neither was the hotshot NHL player who has a rap sheet of conquests and also happens to be my brother's best friend.

I've spent the last three days locked in my house, making the most important decision of my life. Was I going to be a mother? Would I even be a good one? How would I know what to do? Would it come naturally, or would I screw it all up? What would even happen to my career?

Losing my career, and myself was the most terrifying thing I could imagine after what it took to make it here. But I was raised by the best woman in the world, so I'd like to think that somewhere along the way, I got those characteristics from her. I mean, I love Evan with all my heart and then some.

That's when I decided that even if it changed my life, even if it was going to be hard, I was having this baby. No matter what.

With or without Graham.

I'd be a badass lawyer and an even better mom.

"I'm so scared to mess this up." I sniffle, my head in Holland's lap as she strokes my hair. "I mean, isn't this supposed to be a happy, joyous moment? I feel like I'm already fucking things up."

Holland laughs quietly. "There's no manual on how things should go, Em. This is shocking to you because it was never part of your plan. You made a hard decision, and now, you're trying to come to terms with being a mama. No one said it was going to be easy."

Thankfully, telling my best friend was the easiest thing in the world, just like I knew it would be. The rest? I'm not so sure at all.

Looking up at her, a tear slips free. "I mean... you're going to be a great mom, and there's never been any question about that. You were meant to be a mom. Me? I was meant to be the cool aunt that lets the kids stay up late and snort pixie sticks off the coffee table until midnight. I've always put my career first. My happiness first. Now, that's going to change."

She shakes beneath my back, covering her mouth. "You are such a nut. You will be a great mom, Em. The best mom. You'll be kind, compassionate, honest, and loving. You learn, and you grow as you go. You think I had any clue of what to do with Evan? Hell no. He taught me everything. He's taught me patience. How to handle situations with a level head. It's happened, babe, you are pregnant, and unless you know how to rewind time, that is not changing."

I haven't even told Mama or Reed yet. I can't, I'm just not

ready. I'm still trying to come to terms with things myself, and to be honest... how do I tell her "Oh, by the way, I got knocked up by my enemies-with-benefits situationship."

I'm in a *situationship*. That's what it is. A situation where I don't know what the fuck is going to happen, with a man who probably can't even commit to one brand at the grocery store, let alone being a father.

Groaning, I squeeze my eyes shut. "What do I do about Graham?"

"Honestly? Graham will be an amazing father. Truly."

My eyes fly open. "You think?"

She nods. "He's amazing with kids. Olive and Evan are both obsessed with him. He's going to be there for you; I have no doubt."

A series of butterflies, the traitors, erupt in my stomach at the thought of having a baby... an actual child. With Graham.

God, he would be the hottest dad. An Adonis with a baby.

Not that I'll ever, literally ever, admit that out loud.

Holland's right. It does bring some comfort, knowing he will probably be a kick-ass dad, and at least I won't be alone, trying to figure out how the hell to be a parent.

"I'm going to be a mother," I say out loud.

"You are."

"I'm going to be a badass mother, with great tits and even better fashion sense all while being a kick-ass lawyer."

"Yep."

"Okay."

Saying it out loud doesn't make me believe it any more, but I believe in manifestation and we're manifesting this. I can be a badass mother. I *will* be a badass mother. Holland's advice hit home, I *am* pregnant, so it's time to put on my highest heels, raise my chin a little higher and figure this shit out.

First things first... I have to talk to Graham. If we're actually going to do this thing, you know, raise a baby together, there has to be a clear, concise plan.

Ugh, how in the hell am I going to raise a baby with Graham Adams?

It's all fun and games when he's railing you from behind with your hair in his fist, until you're pregnant with his kid.

Glancing in the mirror, I turn sideways and peer at my stomach. I flatten the t-shirt over the span of skin. I'm probably only around fourteen-ish weeks, if my calculations are correct, but soon... this belly will be huge.

I groan, dropping my head to stare at the ceiling. I'm so out of my element.

My first year as an associate and I'm going to be taking an extended period of time off for maternity leave.

I'm spiraling. Again.

I suck in a deep breath, willing myself to calm down and take it one step at a time.

Graham will be here any second to talk, and the sooner it happens, the sooner we can move forward and start preparing. Moving from my bedroom to the kitchen, I open the pizza box and pull out a greasy, cheesy piece of pepperoni pizza and take a bite. I should wait for Graham, but... I need energy. The flu knocked me on my ass, and I've only been feeling slightly better the last few days, and I think that has everything to do with the baby.

Ten minutes later, I hear him knock. I suck in a deep, calming breath and open the door, holding a slice of pizza in my other hand.

He's leaning against the door frame, wearing dark, ripped

jeans and a burgundy t-shirt that hugs his arms, making me slightly turned-on.

Bad Emery. No.

"Hey Em," he drawls. His southern accent peeking through slightly.

"Hi, come in. There's pizza on the counter if you're hungry. You guys had practice, right?"

He nods. "Fucking starving. All I want after practice is food."

"You're just like Reed. He used to eat my mom out of house and home after days on the ice. My mom used to say that she was going to have to put a lock on the pantry because of all his late-night raids. Apparently, it's still a thing."

Graham walks through the living room into the kitchen and pulls out a slice of pizza then takes a huge bite. His eyes roll back and he moans. "Jesus fuck, that's so good. I don't normally eat bad shit, but off-season is happening which means I can splurge… a little."

I nod, shuffling from one foot to the other.

"So…" I say.

"Sooo…" he responds through a mouthful of pizza, "you're having my baby."

Stupid butterflies. My stomach flips and turns at that sentence, and I inwardly curse myself for liking it even the slightest bit.

"I am having *our* baby."

He puts the pizza slice down and walks over to me, then pulls me to him and kisses me before I can even blink. His mouth crushing mine and his tongue dancing along the seam of my lips. It takes a second for me to come to my senses before I push him away, panting.

"What the hell, Adams!"

Laughing, he walks back over to his pizza. "I am so fucking happy."

"You're... happy?"

This is unreal. He's the human version of a golden retriever. I'm convinced.

"Of course I am, Em. You're having my baby. I was nervous at first, then I took some quiet time, reflected on it, and I'm convinced that fate brought us together just for this reason."

I bring my hands to my head and massage the ache that's begun to form in my forehead.

"Quiet time," I repeat.

He nods, shoveling more pizza in his mouth. "I mean, I'm going to have to move in here because I was rooming with Hudson and Asher since we're all bachelors, but it's fine, I think you have plenty of room for all three of us."

"Pause. Hold on. You are not moving into my house, Graham. You're insane, this is insane. Backtrack."

I walk over and take the slice of pizza he's about to put in his mouth, setting it on the box. "Focus. We're not moving in together. I need you to be serious right now, Graham, this is our kid and our future."

"What makes you think I'm not being serious? I'm being one hundred percent serious, Em. Why not? I'll pay the rent, and we'll both be there for the baby."

"Bec- I mean, because we can't just move in together! People don't just do that. Decide they're going to move in together, without even knowing each other."

Rolling his eyes, he steps closer. "I mean, I know you well enough to know what you taste like."

My cheeks immediately heat at the dirty words coming from his mouth. "Jesus. Stop. Okay, we need to sit down and come up with a plan that's thought-out and practical for us both."

This time he throws his head back and laughs and then snatches the pizza off the box and takes another ridiculous bite. "You and your plans. You do realize that there is no plan when it comes to kids; they kind of just do their own shit. It's gonna be okay, Em. You're going to be the best mother, and we'll figure shit out as we go."

"We will not just… figure shit out." I do air quotes around that ridiculous statement because he's obviously insane. I'm having a child with a crazy person.

"Well, I know one thing."

"What?"

"We've got to get married."

Oh. My god. What in the *hell* have I gotten myself into?

I don't even respond, I just leave him standing in the kitchen, stuffing his face with deep-dish pizza, while I seem to be the only sensible, rational person here.

Get married.

"You're being a dick," I say exasperatedly. "This is our future, Graham. Please be serious."

He looks offended. "I am not being a dick, and I am being serious."

I cross my arms over my chest and raise my eyebrow.

"Okay, I realize I probably should have said that a bit more tactfully, but seriously, Em, do you know anything about my family?"

His honey colored eyes, deep and dark, search mine, and I can tell he's serious.

"Aside from the fact that you're from somewhere in Tennessee? No, I don't Graham."

Finally abandoning the pizza, he walks over to where I'm

standing and leans against the counter before continuing, "I'm from a small town in Tennessee, and I was raised by my mama on our family's farm. We provide milk to a huge region in lower Tennessee. My dad passed away of a heart attack when I was eight."

"I'm sorry."

I am. I heard that from Reed once before, I think that Graham was raised by his mom, but I didn't know his father had died. I guess that's one thing we have in common. Probably the only thing. I mean, my father isn't dead, he was just never actually a father to me.

"My mom and my younger sister were all I had growing up. She raised my sister to be strong, independent and I was proud to be raised by a woman like her. Ma taught me to respect women, to work hard, and to never give up on my dreams. I spent more time working on the farm than I did doing anything else. It was my job, my responsibility. If I wanted to have food on the table, I had to step up. My mom and sister couldn't do it by themselves. Even at eight, I became the man of the house. My family is... old-fashioned."

Old-fashioned.

"As in, my mama would beat my ass with a broom if she found out I was having sex outside of marriage, and especially if it was outside of even a relationship. We have to get married, Em, or she's going to actually kill me dead." He looks at me with pleading eyes.

He is one hundred percent serious.

I want to laugh because this situation is honestly that comical.

He's crazy. It's official, without a doubt.

"Graham, that's *not* a reason to get married. Because your

mama will kill you, and because your family is old-fashioned. We're not in nineteen eighteen anymore."

"You don't understand. Everything I've done in my life; I've done for her. Hell, it's the reason I even play professional hockey. I'm here because she made me follow my dreams, and I can't stand to let her down."

My headache is intensifying with each passing second, and it's probably because I've only had that slice of greasy pizza today.

"Can we talk about this later?" I ask, rubbing my temples. I'm overwhelmed right now, even more now than earlier.

He looks like he might say something again, opening then closing his mouth, but then nods. "I know you're overwhelmed, but you're not alone, Em."

"Thank you. I have my first appointment, uh, Monday. If you want to come."

Graham's face lights up, and I see exactly what Holland meant. Graham *is* going to be a great dad, despite his man-whore tendencies, he's kind, and caring, and...good. I've seen it with Evan and Olive. I've seen the loyalty he's shown his teammates and his friends. He's been attentive to me and nice, when I truly didn't give him a reason to be. I'm a big enough person to admit that while I would never date him, he's actually an okay guy.

And the only way I'm going to survive this with my heart in one piece is to make sure it stays in the gilded cage I've built and keep him out. At all costs.

"Of course I wanna be there, Em. I wouldn't miss it for anything. Just text me the time, and where to meet you and I'll be there."

"Okay, glad we got this out of the way. I also have a huge case at work that I've been handed, and I have a lot of pressure on my shoulders, so my schedule will probably be really busy, and-"

"Davidson," he says, interrupting me.

I didn't even realize I was rambling until he stopped me. I've been doing that a lot lately.

"Look, I like you. I like being around you, and I like the fact that you're having my baby. It's not just because my mom will kill me or that I don't want to disappoint her. The ball is in your court, just know that I'll be here regardless."

GRAHAM

TEN

THERE'S a life-size uterus diagram on the wall right in front of me. Complete with all the inner workings, including the birth canal. Which Emery made sure to inform me is exactly where I stuck my dick.

And now… I'm rethinking my entire life.

Cocking my head to the side, I read the small wording next to the arrows on the diagram that point out the medically correct name.

Fallopian tube.

Interesting.

"You are far too interested in that thing." Emery sighs. Her arms are crossed over her chest, pushing her already growing breasts against the thin fabric of her t-shirt. It's been too long since I've touched her, and I'm fucking losing my mind.

I mean, it's not like I ever stopped wanting her, but now with the baby, everything is different.

She's moody, yet I can see her check me out when she thinks I'm not looking. I'm biding my time and waiting for my hot-as-fuck baby mama to cave and give us what we both want. Until then, I'll respect her request for space.

"It's interesting. I've never actually seen the inside. How does a baby... fit in there?"

"Davidson," a nurse calls, appearing from behind the door leading to the exam rooms.

I stand with Emery, suddenly nervous as fuck. I've had time to process the fact that we're going to be parents, but it's so much more real when you're standing next to plastic uteruses, and there's a step-by-step diagram of a water birth playing on the tv.

My throat feels a bit tighter as I take a rough, shaky inhale of breath. We follow behind the nurse into the long white hallway lined with awards with Dr. Ronald Brown's name.

Thankfully, this guy's name precedes him. He's an award-winning gynecologist that comes highly recommended. Emery spent hours reading reviews and looking at their certifications before she booked an appointment. I'm still nervous as hell, no matter how many credentials the guy has.

Finally, we're led into a room off the far end of the hallway. It's bright white, like the rest of the hospital, but decorated with florals. I take a seat opposite the exam table, and while the nurse and Emery are talking, I take a closer look at the paintings.

Wait...

"Those are vaginas." Emery says quietly.

My eyes widen. Holy fuck, they are. They're painted into the flowers like they are blooming from them.

Wow.

"I'm impressed."

"Women are a work of art. It's actually amazing what a woman's body can do." She says.

I drag my gaze from the flower vagina to Emery, who's holding onto a paper gown. "I've seen firsthand how amazing women are. My ma is the best one I know."

She nods. "She sounds like an amazing woman." Averting her gaze, she steps behind the tall curtain to change into the gown, and then reappears a few seconds later with it barely closing behind her.

"This has to be the most unattractive thing to ever grace my body."

"Nah, you could wear a trash bag and still be the hottest woman in the room."

That earns me a small smile, and I'll fucking take it. Emery's beautiful without it, but when she smiles... My heart pounds against my chest, desperate for more.

She hops back up onto the exam table and swings her feet, clad in hot pink socks, back and forth.

"It's going to be weird. Telling all of our friends and family we're having a baby together."

"I don't know. I think they'll probably be shocked but then excited. The guys have always supported me, no matter what it is."

A hard knock vibrates the door, causing us both to glance at the man walking through it. He's older, with gray hair and a clean-shaven face, with a pudgy stomach, and red, rosy cheeks.

He looks like fucking Santa Claus minus the beard.

"Hi Ms. Davidson, I'm Rodney Brown. I hear congratulations are in order." He smiles so big, that I can't help but grin back.

"Thank you. I'm a bit nervous honestly."

He nods. "Of course. Most first-time mothers are, but I'm here to reassure you that you are in the best hands and my staff and I will do everything we can to make sure you are comfortable and feel secure in your pregnancy. That's our job."

Emery nods, still looking nervous in her paper gown, as she chews her lip.

"Alright, I see you think you are about fourteen weeks along, based on your last date of intercourse, but I'd like to go ahead and do an ultrasound to help me determine your due date, and to check the heartbeat and growth of the baby. Lie back here for me, please." He gestures to the exam table, and then grabs a wand attached to a cord from the machine next to him. The lights dim, and he turns the ultrasound machine on.

"This might be a bit cold," Dr. Brown warns before squirting a jelly-like substance on Emery's exposed stomach. "Keep watching the screen and you'll get to see a glimpse of your little baby."

My stomach is tight with nerves. Holy fuck.

I'm about to see my baby for the first time ever. Really any baby, ever, on a screen.

I wipe my sweaty palms on the front of my jeans, taking a gulp of air.

A steady whoosh sounds on the screen, beating in rhythm.

"There's the heartbeat," Dr. Brown says, "strong and steady. Just what we like to hear."

Glancing at Emery, I see tears wetting her cheeks, so I reach out and take her small, clammy hand in mine and squeeze gently, letting her know that she's not alone.

"Hmm," he says.

"What?"

Silence meets my question, and I begin to worry. Is Em okay, the baby?

"Well Emery... It looks like you're having two babies. Twins."

THE SCORECARD

Emery jackknifes from the exam table, sitting up so abruptly, she almost falls completely off it exclaiming, "What? That's impossible."

"Fuck yes," I say, jumping up and pumping the air. "Two!"

Two babies to love instead of one? This is the best day of my fucking life.

Dr. Brown laughs, shaking his head. "Do twins run in either of your families?"

I think about my family tree, realizing we have none on my side, so I shake my head.

"No, I don't believe that we have any twins in my family. God, I was nervous for one baby, but two.... How? I mean, how can we be having twins?" Emery says, rubbing her temples.

"Lean back and let me take a further look. If neither side of your families has twins then this is pretty rare. If my hunch is right, then you might be having identical twins."

Emery croaks, flopping back on the table, and I grin wider.

I can't wait to tell Ma and Allie. I hope they're boys.

Twin fucking boys.

"Em, this is amazing."

Another croak.

"Yes, it looks like they are identical. Do you see right here? They are sharing the same sac. This is pretty rare as far as twin pregnancies go, and this type of twins is referenced as monoamniotic. This can sometimes be dangerous because one twin can essentially steal blood and nutrients from the other, but you are very early along and we will monitor you closely. In some cases, they can separate and each have their own sac. They do seem to each have their own placenta to protect them, which is good news."

"Identical twins?" Emery says roughly.

Dr. Brown nods, giving her a smile before moving the wand

around again over her jelled stomach. "That means you are either having two boys or two girls. Since they are identical, you can't have both. Monoamniotic twins make up less than one percent of babies."

"So, my babies are one of a kind." I smirk. Pffft, and I was number five on that stupid scorecard. Obviously, I deserve the top spot. Identical freaking twins.

"Yes, you could say that." He laughs. "Alright, see here is baby A and then right here is baby B."

He's using his finger to point out the two tiny little beans on the black and white screen of the ultrasound machine. I say beans because they seem to be bouncing around like jumping beans.

My baby beans.

I think I'll call them that.

"When can we find out what they are?" Emery asks. Her eyes are still wide with panic and her body tight with tension.

"Generally, around eighteen weeks. With twins, we generally put you in the high-risk category because twin pregnancies can be a bit more complicated. That means more appointments and ultrasounds, but other than that, you should be perfectly fine. We will keep a close eye on them with bi-weekly ultrasounds around your twenty-week mark, but once a month until then unless there are any problems."

Emery nods, exhaling. "And... normal activities are okay?"

Her eyes dart to me and then back to Dr. Brown, while her cheeks turn a rosy, red even in the dim room.

"If you mean sex, then absolutely. Contrary to the myth that circulates, sex is not going to harm your baby in any way. It's healthy, and great for your body as a stress reliever. You will probably have a much higher sex drive while pregnant. There are hormones running haywire in your body right now, so if you see an increase in libido, listen to your body."

So, what he's telling me is that my hot-as-sin baby mama is going to need my dick even more than she did to put us in this situation.

Fuck yeah.

"Thank you."

The Dr. nods. "If you have any questions at all, you can reach me on this number." He hangs the ultrasound wand up and reaches into his pocket and produces a business card. "This is my direct cell number and you can reach me night or day. I'll print a few pictures of the babies for you to keep and be sure to take your prenatal multivitamins every day. The girls at the front desk will schedule you for three weeks out. In the meantime, call me with any concerns."

Once he's done printing the black and white ultrasound photos, he gives Emery something to clean the jelly off her stomach with, then turns to me and extends his hand. "Congratulations to you both. I look forward to next time."

"Thanks Doc."

"Thank you," Emery whispers, sitting up.

Once he's gone and the door is shut behind him, Emery speaks.

"This is crazy. Insane. Of course, you'd knock me up with not one kid but *two*."

I shrug. "Can't deny fate, babe."

The smile on my face only widens at her annoyance. Fuck, she's adorable.

Groaning, she sits up, pulling the paper gown down. "This is something that would happen to me."

"It just means two babies to love, instead of one. I have lots of love to give."

For a second, her face softens. She picks up the photos Dr. Brown printed and looks at our baby beans.

"Two. For God's sake, I hope they are girls."

"Nah, they're definitely going to be boys."

We laugh together, the first, since all of this happened, and it makes my chest feel lighter.

"Either way, I just want them to be healthy. Ya know?"

I nod, reaching out and taking her hand. I squeeze it gently to reassure her. We're going to be okay. Everything is going to be okay.

"Well... now we tell our families."

Now this will be good.

EMERY

ELEVEN

"TWINS?" Reed exclaims, leaping from the couch. "Wait, what? What do you mean twins? You're *pregnant*?" He begins pacing the room, pulling on his mop of curls while he tries to come to terms with what we've just announced.

"Well, I mean generally having twins means you are pregnant bro." I say.

He stops pacing to look at me, "Sorry if I'm in fucking shock that my best friend knocked up my baby sister. Wait, wait, wait. *Is my sister your Tuesday hookup?*" He looks like he's about two seconds from stalking across the room and killing Graham.

I'm going to die of mortification. *Jesus.*

"Fuck no, she is not. I'm not hooking up with anyone for your information." Graham says to Reed, shooting him daggers with his eyes.

"Good, I'd hate for my nieces or nephews to be fatherless because I had to kill him."

I roll my eyes, while Holland shakes her head, stifling a grin at my brother's reaction to the news.

"Oh my god," my mother cries, covering her mouth as tears well in her eyes. "My baby is having babies!"

Trust me when I say, I didn't actually plan to have everyone here at once, dropping this kind of bomb, but Graham said it's like a Band-Aid, and we needed to rip it off and get it over with.

And... he's probably right.

So, here we are. In my living room surrounded by our family and friends, less of Graham's, of course, since they're in Indiana, or Idaho or wherever they are.

We'll cross that bridge once we cross this one. I'm taking it one day at a time.

"So, you two have been secretly banging? Wow, and I thought you hated each other." Hudson smirks, looking between the two of us.

"Well, I'm pretty sure she still hates me, but here we are," Graham says.

I reach over and punch him in the arm, not hard, but enough to sting.

"What the hell was that for, Em?"

"Don't be crass. Either of you." I narrow my eyes at Hudson, who raises his hands in surrender. "I'm pretty sure we're all adults here and we know exactly how babies are made since you all have them. Yes, Graham and I are having babies together. Two. Twins, and they are identical from what we know right now."

"*Identical twins*," Reed squeaks, his eyes wide, "I feel like I missed a chapter. Fuck, I'm in the wrong goddamn book."

Holland shoots him a death stare and yanks on his hand, pulling him back down to sit.

"I know it's shocking, we're pretty shocked too, but we're having babies. And there's no going back. So, we just wanted to tell all of you together. This is a... complicated situation. We're not together romantically but we *are* going to work together to raise the babies."

"Sound familiar?" Briggs nudges Maddison, who's trying to wrangle Olive, their toddler from knocking over my bookshelf.

Maddison laughs, nodding. She clutches her belly lovingly, rubbing the protruding bump. Kind of ironic that Holland, Maddison and myself are all pregnant. At the same time.

Honestly, it makes me feel marginally better about being pregnant for the first time. Knowing I'll have the best support system in the world.

"I'm just ready for all this baby shower food," Asher quips.

"Yeah, dude, same, they always have those little BBQ weenies," Hudson agrees. "Oh hell yeah, and cupcakes."

"Fuck yeah, those are my favorite. We're definitely having those, right Em?"

Jesus Christ.

"Will all three of you be quiet?" Reed grunts. "I just found out my baby sister is pregnant, and you fuckers are worried about BBQ weenies and baby showers. Em, are the babies going to be okay? Are you okay?"

The entire time he's speaking, he's pacing the floor, running his hand through his already tousled hair. Something I've seen him do a hundred times.

"I'm going to fucking kill you Adams." He says, clenching his jaw. Reed's worried, and I can tell by his reaction, and I don't blame him. My heart jumps against my ribs at the sincerity in his eyes. My brother's always been my protector, my go-to guy when the world was falling apart, and I know now, even though we're both adults, he's still that man in my life.

"Yes, we're all fine. The doctor does want to monitor me closely, especially because the twins-"

"Baby beans," Graham interjects.

"Shut up, dickhead. You knocked up my baby sister. The best thing you can do is stay over there and shut up." Reed grunts at Graham, who only smirks.

I put my hand up and raise my voice to talk over the manly shit happening right now. "The babies are sharing the same sac, making them monoamniotic, and there is a risk with that. I've done some research, and I'm hoping that there is a membrane separating them, but it's just too early to tell. Other than that, Dr. Brown thinks I should have a normal, healthy pregnancy."

Reed nods then stalks over to Graham. "I can't believe you touched her."

"Reed, it wasn't like I set out to sleep with your sister." Graham lowers his voice, so it's barely above a whisper. "I care about her. I do. I promise I'll do right by them."

Swallowing down the emotion clogging my throat, I sit next to Holland.

My best friend has tears in her eyes as she takes my hand and squeezes. "I can't believe that we're all pregnant together. I mean, I can, but it's just so crazy!"

"Me either, Holl. I'm nervous, and scared, and honestly, I feel like I might suck at this, but I'm...excited."

Mom stands from the couch and walks over, taking me into her arms, holding me tightly against her body. I slide my arms around her and don't let go.

It's always been my mom and Reed. Just the three of us, and then Holland and Evan joined our family. My father has never been present in either of our lives, but most of the time, his presence isn't ever missed.

Reed and Mom made sure I had a happy and loved childhood.

"I know you're nervous, baby, but you will be an amazing mother. I'll be here every step of the way," Mom reassures me.

I nod in her embrace.

"So, who's hungry?" Graham asks, breaking the silence and heavy tension in the room. Reed still looks like he might have an actual coronary, but less red than he was a few minutes ago.

Now that my family knows, I feel much better. It seems like I might actually be able to do this.

Everyone begins to get their plates, and it's like the news that we just dropped on them is now just a part of life. The guys talk sports, the girls talk baby stuff, and soon, they're all getting ready to head out.

Reed, Holland and Evan walk out the front door, and he looks back over his shoulder, "I'm still thinking about murdering you."

Later that night, after everyone has gone home, and I'm alone, lying in bed eating peanut butter with a spoon, my phone vibrates with a call.

Glancing at the screen, Graham's name pops up. I groan around the spoon in my mouth.

"Hello," I answer.

"Hello, my beautiful, smart, selfless, best tits in the universe, baby mama."

Suspect.

"What do you want, Adams?"

A brief pause before he speaks again, "Well, I'm choosing to discuss this on the phone instead of actually in front of you, because I think you might kick me in the dick, and you know how much I value my dick."

"Okay.... go on."

"We need to go visit my family and tell them the news in person. I can't tell them over the phone, and now that it's the off-season, I promised my mom that I would visit for a few weeks."

If the spoon of peanut butter wasn't in my mouth, I would've dropped it.

"Graham, I can't just... take off from work and go stay on your family's farm for a few weeks. Plus, I don't think now is the time for me to meet the family. God, this is so complicated."

"Listen, Em, it's important to me, okay? It matters to me, even just meeting them. You're important to me."

His words hit me straight in the heart, and I groan out loud. "Stop tugging on my hormonal pregnant heart strings, Adams. Truly, I don't think I can. You know this huge case just landed in my lap, and honestly, I'd rather endure fifteen vaginal exams than be on a plane with you for an extended period of time."

"What you really mean to say is wow, Graham, your cock is so huge, and I love when you do that thing with your tong-"

I'm tempted to end the call, because it would serve him right, but instead, I lie, "If only that was true, I wouldn't be using my trusty friend BOB."

He tries to speak, but I continue, "I'll talk to my boss tomorrow about working remotely, but I can't make any guarantees, and let me be clear, the only reason I'm even considering this is for the twins, and because of your mama."

I hear his sigh of relief through the speaker.

"Thank you, Davidson, even though you just lied to my face about how great my cock is. There's also one more tiny thing..."

Silence hangs through the line.

"What?"

"I kind of accidentally slipped up and told her we're engaged."

This time my jaw flies open and the spoonful of peanut butter falls into my lap. "You did what!" I screech. "Have you lost your damn mind?"

"I know, but she just made me feel like shit, without actually trying to make me feel like shit, and I panicked alright, I fucking panicked, and now she thinks we're engaged, and I am not going to be the one to tell her that I lied, and neither are you, if you want to have a father for your kids that's not a gravestone."

My god, this keeps getting worse and worse by the second.

I don't even *like* Graham Adams, how in the hell do I pretend to want to *marry* him?

"I'm punching you in the face when I see you."

He laughs, unaffected by my threat of bodily harm. "I'll gladly take it. If you do this favor for me. I just... I can't disappoint her, Emery. Please do this for me, and I'll be on my best behavior."

Sighing, I mull over his request. I don't know how we will pull this facade off either way, but I don't want Graham to get caught in a lie.

He's an idiot. But, he's an idiot with good intentions.

"I'm not saying that I'll do this. And I don't even know if I *can* work remotely or take time off. And even if I did say yes, and I was going to help you cover your enormous lie out of the goodness of my heart, I am not a country girl, Graham. Mud and bugs freak me out."

A loud timbred laugh floats through the phone, warming my insides, which I promptly ignore, reminding myself that his charm is what got us into this situation in the first place.

"Babe, I'm not asking you to muck stalls. Just meet my mom

and sister, pretend we're happily engaged when we spill about our little beans. Get it, spill the beans. I'll be forever in your debt."

"First, don't call me babe. Second, if and only if I agree to this, I'm not even sure that I can pretend that hard, Graham."

He sighs, long and hard. "It's not like we're going to be full-frontal PDA. Just think about it, okay? Know that it would mean a lot to me."

"Alright. I'm headed to bed. I have to have the meeting with my boss tomorrow about the twins and my stomach is in knots. I'll bring up the working remote thing or taking time off. It's not like I've taken a vacation in all of the years I've worked for him, so there's a possibility. But *I'm not saying yes, okay?*"

"Done. Sleep well... *babe*."

I end the call and pick up the dropped peanut butter spoon from my lap, contemplating how I ended up caught in this tangled, annoyingly complicated web with Graham in the first place.

Oh yeah, the stupid scorecard, which led to his magic cock.

Which I refuse to think about, and now... I'm thinking about it. At this rate, my battery-operated boyfriend is going to run out of juice in a week.

I'm a single, hot, independent woman with a kick-ass career and I'm resorting to using to my BOB because I've taken a vow of abstinence from my very hot baby daddy, whose muscles have names I don't even remember, and who, without even trying, has me ready to rip my underwear off and toss them at him.

If that's not a complicated situation, I don't know what is.

A couple weeks pass in the blink of an eye. At least that's what it feels like. One night I went to bed and I swear, the next morning, I woke up with a baby bump. Or babies, in this case.

Probably not actually overnight, but it feels that way.

I've spent the last few weeks trying to process all the changes in my life, to my body, to my relationships. Because it feels like all of these changes are changing me too.

I woke up an extra hour early today to get in a yoga class at the gym, which made me feel so much better, and then I took my time getting ready for work. Today is a big day.

I've spent the last seven years preparing for my career. Studying to pass the bar, planning everything in my life around becoming a lawyer for Johnson and Montgomery. I've sacrificed, I've put in my blood, sweat, and tears, and now I'm finally a first-year associate, with a bright future ahead.

And now I'm pregnant with *twins*. Not one, but two.

I'm terrified that everything I've been working so hard for will take a back burner. To raising babies. Bottles, diapers, playdates, then becoming a soccer mom… and that's just not the life I ever pictured for myself. It's part of the reason why I didn't want a family or children to begin with, because I've been so focused on my career that there hasn't been a time where I thought children or a family would ever fit in that picture.

Logically, I know I won't be the first lawyer to have kids and still have a successful career; I just don't want to deviate from my ten-year plan. I want to be a senior partner by the time I'm forty, and somehow, I still have to make that work and also be a great, devoted mother.

Sighing, I curl another piece of my chestnut hair until I've finished my whole head. I run a wide-tooth comb through the tight curls, loosening them into a relaxed wave. I go light on the makeup, and pair it with my favorite pencil skirt, blouse and pair of black Louboutin.

God, will I still even be able to wear my favorite patent-leather pumps when I have cankles and a stomach the size of a basketball?

Stop being selfish, Emery, I tell myself as I put on my lip gloss and then walk to the kitchen for my briefcase but pause in front of the long mirror leaning against the wall in my room.

My stomach protrudes slightly against the silk of my blouse. Putting my hand there gently, I talk to the babies like they'll actually be able to hear me.

"Alright little ones, I need you to make your mama brave today. Wish me luck, because I'll probably need it."

Silence meets my request, but I still smile all the same.

I grab my briefcase and am out the door with a smile still on my face.

My office is only a couple blocks from my house, so I decide to walk today. Passing by my favorite coffee shop, I stop in my tracks when I realize that the only thing that got me through law school and preparing for the bar is something I'll be giving up during pregnancy.

"Hi, what can I get you?" the smiling barista asks as my eyes scan the menu.

"Uh, whatever pregnant women can have?"

She laughs. "How about your normal order and we can make it decaf?"

I nod. At least I can still have coffee… minus that caffeine that I've spent the last five years surviving on. For good measure, I order Rob one and then finish the short walk to work.

The building is bustling the second I step through the large grand foyer entrance and take the elevator up to my floor. It seems like everyone is in a hurry to go absolutely nowhere, and maybe they always had, but today just feels different.

I guess I'm noticing now because there are other bigger things happening in my life. Causing me to stop and look at things differently.

It's crazy how one thing can change the entire course of your life.

The elevator dings, signaling I've arrived at my floor, and I get off, holding both coffees.

"Em!" my colleague, Amy, says. She's been next to my cubicle for a couple of years, and while we have next to nothing in common, she's always been kind and helpful.

"Hi Amy!" I say cheerfully, plastering a smile on my face.

"Did you hear?"

Her eyes dart around the room as she steps closer and lowers her voice to a hushed tone. "That big time client that Rob is hoping to score? He's here. He popped in for a surprise visit. I'd head straight there if I was you. Good thing you got him a coffee this morning, I hear he's in a mood." She glances down at the cup in my right hand and then gives me a sympathetic look before she scampers back to her desk.

I hardly even have time to set my purse down on my desk when the intercom is beeping.

"Emery, please come to my office now."

Rob clicks off before I can even answer.

Okaaaaay.

I suck in a deep breath, willing my nerves to placate, before I pick his coffee back up and head down the hallway to his office. Through the glass, I see him talking to a guy in his mid-forties, I'd say, short, with dark hair that's tousled. My boss is wearing his "fuck I hate my life" smile, so this should be a great day.

I knock lightly, then enter when he signals for me to come in.

"Good morning." My voice is sing-songy, and I clear it quickly. "I brought you your favorite coffee, Rob."

I place the still hot coffee in front of him on the conference room table and turn to the client.

"Hello, I'm Emery Davidson. It's nice to finally meet you."

"Ah, Emery, Rob told me that I'll be working closely with you on my case. It's nice to finally meet you. My name's Zack." He extends his hand for me to shake, so I do.

"Take a seat Emery," Rob says.

I sit across from Zack and Rob who is next to Camden, who tosses me a quick smile.

"I was just telling Rob that I'm glad we are finally working together. I know you guys mostly handle divorce and family law, but Rob assured me that although this isn't your guys' wheelhouse, you are more than capable of handling the situation."

Nodding, I smile. "Of course. It would be an honor to work together. Rob's said a lot of great things about you."

"Rob and I go way back. We graduated high school together, and our wives have been friends, for hell, a decade at least I'd say. There's one thing you should know about me, Ms. Davidson."

"Please, call me Emery."

His lips tug into a warm grin while he adjusts the button of his suit jacket. "Emery, I'm a family man. I love that Rob and I have a connection that goes beyond business. It makes me more confident in working with him because I truly know the kind of guy that he is. Do you know what I mean?"

I nod.

"It took me a long time to decide to pursue this, and our

connection is what solidified things and made me call this impromptu meeting with his firm. I'm a big family guy, and it's important to me that I do business with a firm that understands those values. I have twin boys, and I'm trying to instill those values in them, even at a young age. Both my wife and I value that connection over everything."

Before I even think about it, the words come tumbling out of my mouth like word vomit. "I completely understand Zack. This is crazy, but my… fiancé Graham and I just found out that we're expecting twins as well."

Rob's eyes go wide, and Zack's face lights up.

"Congratulations! What a blessing. Fate as it may have it. This is exactly what I was just talking to my wife about."

Inwardly, I say a prayer, thanking God for aligning the stars for me here.

"Wow. Can you believe it?"

I glance at Rob, and he nods ever so slightly.

"This is incredible. I believe paths cross for a reason, whether it's professionally or personally. There's a reason for every single person you encounter, every person you meet. This is one of those situations. Without a doubt."

He turns to Rob and claps him on the back. "My man. You know what we should do? We should meet up for dinner. All of us, the wives, Emery's fiancé and Camden's girlfriend too. Before I leave next week for Rome. My treat. We can get to know each other a bit better, and then we can discuss business whenever I'm back."

"Yeah, that would be great. Emery, Camden, would Friday work for you?"

Chewing my lip, I think for a brief second if I have anything planned, except you know, going to Graham's families house this weekend.

"Nope, Friday works for me perfectly."

I smile at Zack who returns it widely.

"Perfect. I'll have my assistant book it, and I'll see you guys then. It was a pleasure to meet you Camden, and Emery, congratulations again. I wish you a healthy, happy pregnancy."

"Thank you so much, Zack." We all rise from the conference table and walk over to the door as Rob and Zack say their goodbyes.

Once he disappears through the glass doors and out into the lobby, Rob says an octave louder, "Twins? You think you could have mentioned that prior to a meeting with the most important client we'll ever have, Emery?"

I shrink back slightly. "I'm so sorry. It seemed like a good time to throw it in there when he was raving about his family."

Rob stalks back to his desk and throws himself in his desk chair and rubs his forehead. "Engaged? Did I miss something?"

Now I see what Graham meant by panicking. My throat feels tight, like it's constricting by the second. God, I feel like I stuffed my foot right in my mouth and now I'm creating an even bigger mess for the both of us.

"Uh, yeah, Graham is the right wing for my brother's hockey team."

Rob's eyes go so wide, they might pop out of his head. "Wait, as in Graham Adams? Number fourteen? The *BEST* rookie player the NHL had ever seen?"

Here we go.

"Yep, that's the one. He's my...fiancé."

"Wow. Well, congratulations. Tell your fiancé I'm a big fan, and I look forward to meeting him at dinner."

I guess it's now or never, swallowing thickly, I ask, "So, I actually wanted to ask you if it would be okay if I take some time off. Graham planned a trip home to his family to tell them the news and asked if I could come along to meet his family. I'll have my computer and access to phone calls and email at all times."

Rob looks down at the desk calendar in front of him then lifts the page. "I don't see why that would be a problem. I think HR could accommodate that if you've got the leave time."

I nod. "I do. Thank you, Rob. I appreciate you letting me do it so last minute."

"It's not a problem. When you get back, hopefully, we will have sealed the deal with Zack and can start working on his case. Did you look over those old case files I sent you?"

"Yes, they're on my desk. I'll go get my notes and come straight back here."

"Thanks."

I give him a slight wave, and turn on my heel to leave, before something happens, and he changes his mind.

God, we're in such deep shit. Graham's lying to his family, and I'm lying to my boss and the biggest client our firm hopes to land, and I'm terrified it's all going to blow up in our faces.

This could end so badly.

I convinced myself that I might actually tell Graham no and that coming clean to his mother was the right thing to do, but now... I've dug us into an even deeper hole.

My hand rubs my stomach absentmindedly as I whisper to the twins, "Well girls, looks like we're in some deep s-h-i-t."

I probably shouldn't assume they're girls, but one can hope. My hands shake as I pull out my phone and pull up Graham's text thread.

Me: May or may not have told my boss that we're engaged and would love to come to dinner with him and a huge potential client on Friday. Pls tell me you're free?

I wait a few seconds as his response bubble pops up.

Graham: Welcome to the dark side, Davidson. I'd be happy to do you this favor, but as you know, favors come at a price.

Rolling my eyes, I respond.

Me: Are you forgetting the fact that you asked me to lie for you first? Or shall we go tit for tat. Be serious Graham, please clear your schedule. I panicked and told him we were free, and of course, he's your biggest fan. You have to come.

Graham: Done. I'll come dressed in my Sunday best… ;) But, we have to figure out how we're going to pull this off. Can I come over tonight?

Me: Yes, but can you stop and get me a pint of chocolate chip cookie dough ice cream? I'm craving something sweet.

Graham: All you had to do was ask, babe, and I've got something sweet to give you.

Me: I hate you.

Graham: See you at seven ;)

Once I make it back to my cubicle, I cross my arms on my desk and drop my head onto them. For what seems like the millionth time this week, I ask myself, *What in the hell have I gotten myself into?*

GRAHAM

TWELVE

FIVE MONTHS AGO, I had a hookup schedule, and now, I'm bringing ice cream to my pregnant baby mama, who answered the door wearing bunny slippers and an old t-shirt with the words Harvard across the front.

Who has never looked fucking hotter.

And now I'm hooked on her.

"Gimmie, gimme," she says, closing the door with her furry pink foot.

I hand her the bag of ice cream, before losing a limb in the process. These hands are worth millions, do you blame me?

"Three?" Her eyebrows raise as she looks inside the paper bag.

"Yup. There were so many to choose from, I got overwhelmed. Look, I don't buy women... ice cream. This is new for me Em, I'm learning."

She pulls the top off of my personal fav, good ole Ben and Jerry, and shoves the spoon in the top and stuffs it into her mouth. With a mouthful of ice cream, she moans around the spoon, closing her eyes shut.

It's an experience.

I should probably be ashamed that my dick stirs to life when she does, but whatever. She's fucking hot, and my dick misses her.

"I can't stop eating. Everything. I'm starving. All. The. Time. I'm going to be as big as a house. Actually my pants aren't fitting anymore so there's that."

"You're growing two babies, *eat*."

She rolls her eyes at my tone, shoveling another spoonful of ice cream into her mouth. "Yes, *Daddy*."

My dick twitches. Fuck.

"I mean..."

Her eyes narrow. "Don't even start."

Smirking, I walk over and take the spoon from her and take the bite she was about to put in her mouth, earning me a punch in the shoulder.

"Gross, you just ate off my spoon, jerk. Germs Adams."

"I've also eaten your pussy so...."

"You're disgusting."

"Call me what you want, but it's true. Which is still very much on the table, you know that right?"

The look she shoots me might actually put me in the ground, so I should probably shut the fuck up, but I continue anyway, because I'm a martyr after all.

"Just saying. You heard what the doctor said, you're pregnant and there are *lots* of hormones coursing through your body. You're going to have an itch that only I can scratch, babe, and I'm at your service."

And I better be the only one touching Emery, because I might lose my shit in the process. I feel this.... Protectiveness that I've never felt with anyone else when it comes to Emery.

Ignoring me, she pushes past me to sit down on her plush

sofa. In doing so, the back of her t-shirt rises slightly, giving me a glimpse of her long, tan legs, making my mouth water.

I follow her to the living room and sit on the opposite side of the couch. She turns toward me and pulls her legs crisscross as she eats.

"First things first, if we're actually going to pull this off, without it being a gigantic clusterfuck and blowing up in our faces, we have to be convincing," she says around the spoon.

She sucks the ice cream off the tip, flicking her tongue along the length of it and swirling it on the spoon to get the remainder off, making it really hard to focus on what she's saying.

"Graham."

"Hmm."

Her eyes roll back, and she stops her assault on the spoon that I'm convinced is solely made to torture me.

Dick. Twitching.

"Focus."

Right, fake engagement.

"I mean, we have chemistry, Em. It's not like that's something we're lacking, *obviously*." I gesture to her now rounding stomach.

Emery can pretend to dislike me all day, but the fact is, we have out of this world chemistry. When we're together, it's like she lets down the barrier around her just a little, and it's just us.

Lately, I've been noticing how her body is changing. Not that she's let me touch her, in what feels like ever, but I've noticed her baby bump becoming more prominent by the day. And God, her tits.

I don't know for the life of me why she's worried about something happening to them because all they've done is gotten bigger and juicer. Like ripe apples I want to take a fucking bite of.

She's sexier now than I've ever seen her, even more so knowing she's got my babies in her belly.

"Okay, but it's more than just chemistry, Graham. For instance, how did we become a couple? Oh God, how did you propose to me? What about a ring?"

She lifts her hand up and wiggles her ringless fingers.

"You let me handle the ring, okay?" She's not picking out her own damn ring, fake engagement or not.

"Fine. How about we just say that we, of course, met through Reed, and then we hit it off. You asked me out, and I turned you down at first. That's believable. Our friends would never believe it, which is fine, we'll keep it to your family only." She grins and takes another bite of that damn ice cream that I'm cursing myself for even picking up.

"Fine. How did I propose?"

Her shoulders dip in a quick shrug. "I dunno."

"How about this: I brought you to the arena, where it all started. Where I saw you for the first time, in the stands. The first time I ever saw you, I thought you were the most beautiful girl in the entire stadium. Thousands of people and all I saw was you. At the time, I didn't even know you were Reed's sister. I just knew that one look and I wanted you. Then, when I realized that you were his sister, I knew I'd never have a chance. I had a better chance with Reed himself than ever getting you. Until we met at dinner that day at Reed's."

Little does she know, everything in that story is true.

The day I saw her in the arena, it was our first home game. My rookie season. I saw her sitting next to Holland, her head thrown back in laughter, her cheeks red with mirth.

It sucked the breath right out of my lungs, like I had been shoved against the boards of an arena.

I said I was going to find her, after the game, when interviews were over and I was showered. Then, she was gone.

I saw her at Reed's for the second time two weeks later, at the first family dinner I'd been invited to. I almost swallowed my tongue, but then I knew better than to pursue her. Hell, Reed would've skinned me alive for even looking at her. Not that she needed to know what I felt in that moment was real. I'm pretty sure at the first sign of anything... too personal, too intimate... she's going to bolt. I'm not going to do anything that jeopardizes how far we've come in just a short time.

Including anything that adds to her phobia of commitment.

Her head nods in agreement. "Yeah, that would work. And, I'm always at games for Reed, so it makes sense. Maybe we bumped into each other afterwards, and you asked me out, and I couldn't resist your charm."

"So, I proposed at the arena, just you and me. I put it on the scoreboard and got on one knee right in front of the very seat I first saw you in." My eyes catch hers.

"That's...romantic."

She looks surprised, her eyebrows raised.

I shrug, giving her a small smirk. "I'm a romantic guy."

She laughs, a sweet sound that echoes off the walls of her living room; it may just be the first genuine laugh I've gotten from her since all of this started. "Oh? Sorry, Adams, you don't peg me as a romantic guy."

"Well, you've never seen me in action. There's plenty of time, babe, don't worry."

Her eyes roll, then she yawns and leans forward to put the ice cream on the coffee table. Stretching her arms above her head, she lets out a breathy moan. "I'm exhausted. I feel like I've run a marathon and I haven't done anything but work."

The thing is... for Emery, I want to be a romantic guy. I want to make her feel special, and fuck, I want to make her feel everything. All the emotions she keeps trying to run from. I want to break down the wall around her heart that she's built up ten feet tall. I've always had a thing for her. I wasn't joking when I said that, I meant it, and I know right now, if I tell her that, then she's going to shut down, and push me away.

But the truth is... I hoped our hookup would turn into more. I didn't want to be the hook up guy any longer. I guess that might make me soft, but I don't give a shit. I want this to be real. I want Emery, me, and our babies to be a real family. I don't just want her to meet my mama, pretending to be engaged; I want to meet her and things between us be *real*.

I'm going to change her mind, no matter how long it takes. I'm going to show her how good we are together.

"Are you busy?"

Emery's voice floats through the phone full of apprehension. "Uh, well it's nine p.m. and I just put on Good Girls, so...yes?"

"Well, could you come somewhere with me? You can wear your pajamas if you want, including the bunny slippers."

There's a thump through the speaker. "Like... right now? At this very second?"

"Yep. I was kinda hoping you'd say yes, so I'm already halfway to your house."

She groans, which makes me smile, because that means she's going to say yes.

After our conversation a couple days ago, I thought about what kind of ring I would get Emery, and while I could probably buy the most expensive ring in Harry Winston, that doesn't mean she's going to like it.

Fake or not, I want her to love the ring she's wearing.

Call it what you will, it's something I'm not changing my mind about.

"This better be good, Adams, Rio is the only man I want to see right now."

Who the fuck is Rio? I make a mental note to ask her as soon as I see her.

When I pull up to her house, walk up the drive, and knock, it only takes her half a minute to open the door. It actually flies open, and she steps out, wearing a tank top and jean shorts, paired with a simple pair of sandals.

Her cheeks are flushed, and she looks like she just crawled out from under the covers. Simply put, she looks so fucking cute I want to bring her right back through that door and give her a real reason to have the flush on her cheeks.

"Hi." I grin.

"Hi. You gonna tell me where we're going?"

"Nope," I gesture to the truck, "but we need to get going or we're going to be late."

She eyes me suspiciously for a moment, but then brushes past me to my truck. Following closely behind her, I reach around and open the door before she can, helping her inside the cab.

Our ride is short, only a few blocks over from her suburbia house. I drive us downtown and find the closest parking garage to our destination.

When she sees where I've brought her, she looks at me with her mouth agape.

"No way. Hell no, Adams. This is not happening."

Smirking, I lace my hand in hers and tug before she can protest. Harry Winston is lit up brightly for this time of night, and when I knock, the manager, Barry, opens the door with a gracious smile and welcomes us inside.

"Mr. Adams, Ms. Davidson, good evening and welcome to Harry Winston."

I shake his hand and glance at Emery, who's chewing on her lip in thought. Her wide blue eyes scan the glass cases of diamonds, and she looks about two seconds from bolting.

Walking over to her, I stand right in front of her and lift her chin with my thumb.

"You need a ring. This is the place to get a ring, Em."

She shakes her head. "Yeah, Harry freaking Winston, Graham? God, these rings probably cost more than my house. Did you rent out the entire place just for this?"

"Would pretending that I didn't make you feel better?"

She groans, dropping her head into her hands and covering her face. "This is too much. You're doing too much."

"Remember when you said that we had to make this believable? Well, no one would believe that I bought you a ring that wasn't worthy of you, Emery Davidson. They wouldn't believe it for a second that I didn't buy you a ring I would want to stare at every day and show off that you're mine.

Her throat bobs as she swallows then looks around once more at the glass cases, and finally nods. "Okay. Okay, fine. This is fine."

I almost laugh at the fact that she's trying to reassure herself because it is fine, and she's not walking out of this building without a ring that I'm proud to have on her finger.

No fucking way.

"Pick one. Whatever you want."

"Graham… I can't just pick out a ring. They're all too expensive."

"Emery, pick out a ring."

I nod at Barry, who walks over and smiles at Emery. "I've picked out some of our most beautiful diamonds for you. What cut do you prefer?"

"If it's okay, could I just look around for a while?"

"Of course, take your time, and I'll be here if you see anything that interests you," Barry says, stepping back and sweeping his arm out to the room.

She looks hesitant at first, but finally walks over to the rings that he's set on the counter and lifts a shaky hand to pick up one of the diamond rings. Her other hand is on her stomach, a habit she's picked up in the last few weeks, and one I can't get enough of.

She admires the ring in her hand, and it's almost like she gravitated directly to it. She rubs her thumb across the top and spins it delicately in her finger, before gently sliding it on her ring finger and inspecting it. I can tell how much she loves it just by the way she's staring at it, with such adoration in her eyes.

Then, her head shakes, and she pulls it off, placing it back on the display.

"Is this it?" I ask, walking over and nodding toward the ring she just put back.

"It's beautiful, but it's huge, Graham."

"Barry, can you tell me about this one?" I ask.

He nods, stepping behind the counter. "This is our *The One Oval-Shaped Diamond Micro-pavé engagement ring*. Each diamond is handpicked and unlike any other. As Mr. Winston has always said, "No two diamonds are the same." The center stone starts at 1 carat, but I believe this one is two carats set in a *Micro-pavé* band."

"How much is it?" Emery asks, glancing down at the ring again.

"This one starts at One Hundred Thousand dollars."

Her face goes slack, and I swear she goes as pale as the white ring setting in front of her. She shakes her head. "Absolutely not. Thank you but no."

Before I can even speak, she's walking away. Fleeing.

"Em, stop."

She shakes her head. "No, this is crazy. You can't spend One Hundred Thousand dollars on a ring, Graham! God, this is insane. We're insane. We're not even really engaged, and that is literally how much a house costs. No." By the time she's finished speaking, her cheeks are flushed, and she's so fucking adorable when she's mad.

So. Fucking. Adorable.

"Don't over think this, Davidson. I told you whatever you wanted, it's yours. Do it for me. Please?"

"I can't, Graham. I literally cannot. Please, please, let's just look at something cheaper."

I can see the panic in her eyes, and it's the only reason I relent.

"Fine, if that's what you want. I told you I want you to pick out whatever you like." Turning to Barry I say, "Can you show us some that are a little cheaper?"

"Way cheaper. The cheapest you have, actually," Emery interjects.

I shake my head. "Em..."

She holds her hand up, stopping me. "That's it, Graham, or I walk out this door. I sincerely appreciate the fact that you want to get me something lavish, but this engagement is fake, and you work hard for your money. Please, just let's pick out the cheapest one they have. Once we're done pretending, I'll give it back, and you can sell it."

The words shouldn't cause lead to form in my stomach, but they do. I don't want her to ever fucking give it back to me.

I know pressing right now will cause her to run, and we'll be back at square one. So, I nod, shoving my hands in my pockets.

Thirty minutes later, we walk out with a one-carat diamond, in the cheapest setting that Harry Winston makes. The entire ride home, Emery stares at the ring on her finger, fidgeting with it until I pull up in her driveway.

I don't think I've ever seen her nervous, not in all of the time that I've known her.

Putting the truck in park, we sit there silently. A minute passes before she speaks, "I appreciate it, Graham. I do. Please don't think that I don't. I just... I can't accept something like that. I can't. This will do the job, and then some. It's more than enough. You are more than enough."

Ignoring the pull in my chest at her words, I nod and get out to open her door then help her out of the truck. We walk side by side to her front door, and she unlocks it and turns the handle to walk in but stops to face me.

"Thank you."

"It's nothing, Em."

She opens her mouth to say something then closes it, visibly swallowing. It's the first moment between us that has felt different. Deeper. Beyond the surface.

"I appreciate it. I appreciate how you wanted to do something so special and selfless. I just don't want to take advantage." She steps over to me and slides her arms around me, in a lingering hug that I feel in my fucking bones. "You are a good man, Graham Adams. I'll see you tomorrow night, okay?"

"Tomorrow."

When the door closes behind her, I walk back to my truck, a part of me wondering what it would be like for things to be real between us.

The other part, wishing that they were.

EMERY

THIRTEEN

TO SAY I'm nervous is the understatement of a century. It might actually take a miracle to pull this off.

"Ready?" Graham asks, poking his head through the doorway of my room and tapping his watch where I'm in front of my vanity, finishing my makeup. I run my fingers through my curls to loosen them. Doing so causes the rock on my finger to catch the light, and it shines brightly.

Lately, there have been so many changes happening, my head is beginning to spin. Graham, finding out I'm pregnant, this... gigantic diamond on my finger. Pretend or not, it's a lot.

So much so that my head has been second-guessing and doubting myself with every corner I turn.

My eyes drift down to the black-fitted dress I have on for tonight. My very first maternity dress.

Truthfully, I thought all maternity clothes would be hideous and do horrible things to my figure, but turns out... I was wrong.

For the first time in months, I feel sexy in my own skin.

I'm growing babies, and I'm badass, at least I feel like it

wearing this dress. Especially seeing Graham's eyes fill with desire as they drag down my body causing a shiver to travel down my spine.

"Can you zip my dress, please? I can't reach it."

He nods, closing the distance between us. I can feel him along my back, sending a flurry of goosebumps along the bare skin of my arms when his breath hits the back of my neck. Hot and teasing, I feel it all the way to my toes.

Our eyes lock in the mirror while he fingers the zipper at the base of my spine. The second his fingers connect with my skin; I almost moan out loud. The doctor was right; my body is a mess of hormones, and one touch from Graham and I'm a puddle at his feet. I haven't been touched by him in months, and I'm tired of fighting my body's attraction to him.

Simply put, I'm horny as hell, and I'm losing my mind.

BOB is no longer doing the job; well, in comparison to my baby daddy, it never really did.

The nervousness I was feeling for tonight's dinner evaporates, replaced by want.

I feel his fingers trail down my back, featherlight and teasing, dancing along my skin. A beat passes, and then it's as if the string of tension holding us together snaps, and with it goes our resolve.

I'm sick of going out of my mind when he walks in the room and seeing his eyes flare as they took my body in, did nothing but make my body hotter.

Practically crawling out of the dress I so carefully picked out, all because Graham Adams is the hottest man on the face of the planet, and honestly, it's not fair.

At. All.

Whipping around, I turn to face him, and he brings his hands to my jaw, cradling it as he takes my mouth fiercely. It's like water in a drought; I craved this. His touch. The intimacy that I only feel when we're together, like this.

He kisses me until I'm a breathless-panting mess. Reaching down, he lifts me off my feet and places me on the vanity behind me, surging forward, parting my thighs as he nestles between them.

I didn't realize how badly I was aching for him until his hands tangled in my hair, angling my mouth to kiss me deeper. His cock pressed against my already soaked pussy. The thin layer of lace separating us is all that remains.

"Fuck, Davidson." He yanks his mouth from mine, his golden-honey eyes searching me.

"Please fuck me," I all but beg.

At this point, I'm not above it. Anything for him to relieve the ache between my thighs.

He drags his thick thumb along my bottom lip, while staring at me so intently, it feels like his eyes might burn right through me.

"Baby, you don't have to beg. Anything you ever want; I'll hand it to you."

I don't think about the weight of his words; instead, I push it down and pull his mouth back to me, while my shaky hands fumble with the button of his slacks, desperate to have him inside me.

Sensing my struggle, he pulls his lips free and quickly pops the button while my feet push at the slacks on his hips. Finally, I drag his zipper downward, and his black briefs, tight and straining with his cock behind them, come into view. My hand closes around his hardness, earning a sharp hiss from his lips as I squeeze him through the cotton.

God, he's so big, and hard, and I want him more than ever.

Logically, I know that falling back into bed with him isn't

the right decision, not when we're trying to navigate these uncharted waters together, but right now, the lust has taken over, pushing away all reason.

"This means nothing," I say quietly, desperate to keep hold of the sense of control I'm clinging too.

"Whatever you say, Em." He doesn't let me think; he simply pulls me to him, bunching my dress around my hips, exposing the bright red thong I'm wearing. "God damnit, you're like every dream I've ever had come true. No fuck that, you're even better."

His thumb finds my throbbing clit and he rubs gently, my back arching closer to his touch.

"So wet. So ready for me. Do you want me to eat this pussy?"

I nod, unable to find words.

His eyes darken and a wolfish grin quirks his lips. "Have you been aching, baby? Wanting me to fuck you, but being too stubborn to ask me to take care of you?"

Dick.

I tear my eyes from him and look away, only for him to grasp my chin with his thumb and turn my head back to him. He's so close his breath fans across my lips. "If we had more time, I'd spend the rest of the night with my head buried between your thighs, but we don't, so this will be quick, but Emery... make no mistake, this isn't over. Not by a fucking long shot."

My clit throbs in anticipation as he roughly pushes my underwear aside, and in one second, he's inside me so deep my toes curl against his hips. He fucks me in earnest, wasting no time, each thrust deeper than the last. All I can do is cling to him as he fucks me, harder, without abandon

"You're so goddamn beautiful, Emery. Your tits are perfect for my hands, your hips made for me to hold. This belly…"

He reaches down and caresses my stomach in a way that has me shivering beneath his touch. There's something… primal about the way he's handling me, and it's the most erotic thing I've ever experienced.

His hands move to my hips as he pulls out, then surges forward, fucking me hard. My back hits the mirror over and over, my vanity shakes, makeup falling off the side as he pounds into me.

I'm so close, so close to the wave of pleasure I've been denying myself to crest.

"I'm- I…" I trail off, squeezing my eyes shut, my nails raking down his back.

When I feel the rough pad of his thumb ghost across my clit, flicking, and then a quick pinch, rough yet gentle, all at once, I fall, clinging to him as the orgasm crests inside me.

"Graham," I whimper.

"That's it, baby, come on my cock like a good girl." His words come out as a growl.

Oh god, his words of praise spur on the ecstasy inside me. My orgasm seems to drag on, aftershocks rocking my body when he pushes deeper and comes, his mouth colliding with mine on a groan as he spurts hot, deep lashes inside me.

We stay just like that, clinging to each other as our hearts slow, and our harsh breath evens out. The intimacy I was craving, blossoming deep in my bones.

"As much as I don't want to do this… if we don't leave now, we're going to be late as fuck, and I don't think that's the impression you were looking for, babe."

My sex-fogged mine jolts, and I begin to pull my dress back in place as he slides out of me. He then disappears into my bathroom and comes back with a warm rag, gently bringing it between my legs, and I wince at the intimacy of it all.

"Em?"

His voice is low and deep, the baritone reaching inside me and caressing.

"Hmm?"

"I want you to think about this for the rest of the night while my cum drips out of you and remember it the next time you want to deprive yourself."

I swallow thickly, knowing that I will.

We arrive at the restaurant five minutes late, but it was well worth it if you ask me. I may feel differently when I see Rob, but right now, I would gladly skip the dinner entirely for another quickie with Graham.

Hormones. Raging.

Graham's obviously thinking much clearer than I am, because right before the waiter leads us to the table, he grabs my hand, squeezing gently. My brain is completely fuzzy because I almost forgot that we had a part to play.

The second Rob comes into view, his wife along side Zack and his wife, I swallow and get ready to put on our show. Although, I'm ninety percent sure it's going to blow up in our faces, at least we can try.

"Emery!" Zack calls, rising from his chair, smiling widely. His wife is a mousy brunette with big glasses that cover most of her face. She's obviously shy, as her eyes barely meet mine when I say hello. "This is MJ my wife, and this must be your fiancé."

"Hi! Nice to meet you. I'm Emery, and yes this is my fiancé,

Graham," I say, looking over at him. He easily falls into a smile, offering his hand to Zack then MJ.

"Graham! The hockey superstar, I hear." Zack laughs, clasping his hand. "Not much of a hockey fan myself, but Rob here could carry the whole damn team with all the knowledge he's got."

Rob laughs, shaking Graham's hand as well. "I'm Rob, Emery's boss. This is my wife, Malinda. Nice to meet you."

"Nice to meet you all as well. When Em told me about wanting to have dinner and how big of a hockey fan you were, I couldn't pass up the opportunity to talk shop."

Rob practically has stars in his eyes. Graham could charm anyone, anytime, without even trying.

Hell, it's how I ended up like this.

And by this, I mean pregnant.

Camden introduces his girlfriend Aria, and then when all introductions are made, we get seated.

I take a seat across from them, Graham pushing my chair in before taking the seat beside me. We give the waiter our drink order, and when he's gone, Zack looks over at me. "So Emery, I hear you're taking some time off to be with Graham and his family?"

I nod. "Yes, we're going to be going to Graham's farm in Tennessee, to tell his mom and sister the news. About the babies." Instinctively my hand moves to my lower stomach. When I glance over at Graham, he's already looking at me, a small smile on his face. "I've actually never been down south and I'm really looking forward to seeing his family."

Zack looks between the two of us. "I love it. My wife's family is actually from southern Louisiana. A bit farther south than Tennessee, but the culture is amazing down there."

"Ah, I have a cousin who's a physical therapist down there.

She actually works with a lot of athletes who have been injured. I believe she lives in the New Orleans area, or right outside," Graham says.

"Small world. MJ's family is from Metairie. A small town outside of New Orleans."

I look at MJ and give her a smile. She tucks her hair behind her ear and nods shyly. It's actually surprising to see Zack with someone so polar opposite to him. He seems to be a complete extrovert, and one that never meets a stranger.

Dinner passes quickly, we're all so caught up in conversation and swapping stories around the table, that most of the restaurant has begun to clear out.

Rob and his wife tell us goodbye, since they've got a sitter with their kids, and Camden and his girlfriend had plans for after dinner, so it was just Zack, MJ, Graham and I left.

As nervous as I was, our dinner was hardly any talk about work, and most of it spent laughing until my sides hurt.

"Honestly, this was so much fun Zack. MJ. Thank you both for having us all for dinner." I say.

Zack waves his hand, dismissing it, "I've loved getting to know everyone. Especially you and your fiancé. I can't remember the last time I didn't actually talk about a project I was working on and laughed this hard."

I nod in agreement.

Graham reaches out on the table, lacing my hand in his and gives me a reassuring smile.

I can't help but think about his whispered words before we left the house… There has been an undeniable ache between my thighs for the remainder of the night. Every time I shifted on the chair; I could feel the evidence of what we'd done only minutes before arriving here.

The way his eyes, molten amber liquid, just darkened signal he's thinking the same exact thing that I am, right now.

"I've been thinking about broadening this project, maybe heading to the west coast with it, but the first stop is getting everyone on the same page."

I nod, "Rob, Camden and I have been working on getting the contracts set up and will start working on filings soon."

Graham looks around the restaurant and back at us, "Man, we cleared the place out Zack."

Sure enough, we're the only patrons remaining, and we'd been so lost in conversation I didn't even realize it.

"Wow. Well, I guess this is where we say goodbye. I'm really looking forward to working together on this Emery. It was nice to meet you, Graham." Zack rises from the table and extends his hand, shaking Graham's. "I hope to see you both soon."

He places his hand behind his wife's back, and she tosses a shy wave over her shoulder, and they leave us in silence.

Before we can even stand, Graham leans in, his lips brushing against the sensitive shell of my ear, "Let's go Davidson. You haven't been able to sit still all night, and I know you're dying for me to make it better."

In the middle of the restaurant, I clench my thighs together.

But I refuse to admit that he's right.

"You wish, Adams."

GRAHAM

FOURTEEN

"MORNING GORGEOUS."

Instead of a response, I get a very unladylike grunt.

I laugh, holding out the decaf iced coffee and still warm cheese danish I picked up from Em's favorite bakery up the street.

I think I'm doing a pretty good job at being a thoughtful guy.

Not that she's even really noticing, seeing as how she answered the door in sweatpants, a baggy t-shirt, her bunny slippers with a wild case of bedhead and only one eye open.

"What time is it?" she says, her voice still hoarse with sleep.

I glance down at my Apple Watch on my wrist. "Almost nine."

Her eyes fly open. "What? No? Oh God, we're going to miss our flight!" she cries, leaving me standing in her doorway as she flies around her apartment, snatching things off the couch and counter.

"It's fine, we've got an hour. Do whatever you need to do."

She pauses, an adorably frustrated look on her face. "Okay,

give me ten minutes to throw the rest of my stuff in my bag, and I'll shower and get ready. Can you grab my pregnancy pillow?"

I nod. "Yep, no problem."

Nodding, she disappears through the doorway, and I hear her moving and bustling around her room. When I walk through the door, she's lying across a suitcase that's literally bursting at the seams.

"Woah, let me do that." I nod toward her stomach. "Gotta be careful of my babies."

She pauses, standing straight. "Right. Yes."

I walk over to the overflowing suitcase, push down and it shuts with ease. For the life of me, I don't understand why she shoved half her wardrobe in here for a two-week stay, but if it makes her feel more comfortable... Fuck it.

Grabbing her suitcase, then the life-size pillow on her bed, I roll it out to the foyer and wait for her to finish showering. While I have a minute, I pull out my phone and send a quick text to my mom and sister in our family group chat, telling them that we'll be leaving shortly, and I can't wait to see them.

I haven't been home in so long, and it will be the first and only time I've ever brought a woman home with me.

I'm worried Ma might have a heart attack from the shock. She's been trying to marry me off to any of the eligible girls in town since I was barely a freshman in college.

"Ready?" Em asks, reappearing from her room. She's dressed in a flowy shirt and sandals, with a matching gold bracelet and necklace. Seeing the diamond shine on her finger does something to me.

A primal, possessive feeling stirs inside me.

Mine.

"Yep, after you." My hand wraps around the handle of the

suitcase as she opens the door and I follow behind her, my free hand on the small of her back.

She locks up and then turns toward the driver parked in front of the house.

"Really?"

I shrug. "Figured you'd be more comfortable in a limo."

Her eyes soften slightly. "Graham, I don't need fancy or expensive. You know that, right?"

I do, but it doesn't matter. I want to spoil her, take care of her as much as she'll let me. Whenever I can.

"I want to make you happy, Em. Fake or not."

I am beginning to hate this, already. The fake bullshit. Because every single second I'm around her, I want to yank her to me and kiss her until she's breathless, reminding her that there is nothing fake about the way we are together.

But I don't. Because the one thing that will scare Emery off is showing her that what I feel is becoming more real by the second.

After we get to the airport, check our bags and finally board the flight with only minutes to spare, Emery seems to relax while my anxiety skyrockets.

I fucking hate flying. More than anything. Heights in general make my stomach plummet and my chest feel tight.

Gripping the armrests of my seat, my knuckles turn white with the force. Panic rises in my throat, and I can feel my chest growing heavier by the second. The same familiar feeling of a panic attack, just like every time I step onto a plane. I try and suck in a deep breath, but it's difficult with my chest so tight.

"You okay?" Her wide blue eyes are filled with concern.

"Uh," I clear my throat as I reach up and wipe the sweat that's formed along my brow away, "I'm a bit afraid of heights.

You know, flying, falling and plummeting to my death. That sort of thing."

Emery bites her lip to stifle a laugh.

The flight attendant's voice comes over the speaker, preparing the cabin for takeoff, and I squeeze my eyes shut.

Fuck, I hope Emery doesn't think I'm a pussy.

Although, right now I *am* being a pussy.

"Graham, you know you're more likely to die in a car wreck than you are in a plane crash? Like, it's statistically proven?"

I nod, my eyes still tightly shut. I'm scared that if I open them, I'll hurl my cheese danish breakfast everywhere, and I can't imagine that Emery wants to spend the rest of the flight covered in puke. The plane lurches as it begins its takeoff, and I groan. Every time I get back on a plane, I remember exactly why I hate flying and it never fails, I always feel this way. Even after fifty-six games a season, my anxiety and my fear get the best of me.

Needless to say, I don't look forward to plane rides, whatsoever.

Slowly, tenderly, I feel Emery pry my fingers from the seat, and her hand slides into my clammy palm. She squeezes gently. "It's okay. I'm here, okay?"

This girl.

I nod, unable to open my eyes, but I mumble a quick thank you.

I can't muster more than that as the plane skids on the runway. I don't open my eyes again until we're in the air and over the ascent, then the flight attendant comes on the intercom to let us know we can unfasten our seatbelts and are free to move around the cabin.

When I do, I look over at Emery, who's wearing a small grin

at the corner of her lips. She's reading a book on her kindle, but glances up at me.

"Feeling better?"

I clear my throat. "Yeah, uh, sorry about that. I'm really fucking bad with flying."

"Hey, we're all afraid of something." She smiles sympathetically, reassurance laced in her words.

Only then do I realize we're still holding hands; her palm clasped tightly in mine. When she sees me looking down at our joined hands, she quickly lets go and brings her hand back to her lap.

"I can feel them moving around, even more now that we've ascended. It feels like a bunch of butterflies erupting." Her hand moves to her stomach, where she rubs her thumb lovingly. "Do you want to feel?"

I nod, swallowing thickly, emotion clogging my ability to form words. This feels monumental, especially with her sharing it with me. She picks my hand up and places it on her stomach, beneath the soft fabric of her shirt.

At first, we just stare at each other while we wait, and then… I feel it.

A light thump against my hand, then another, and another.

"Em, that's our babies," I say hoarsely, "I can feel them."

She nods, pulling her lip between her teeth. "It is."

It's incredible, feeling them move against my hand, and now more than ever, I feel confident that I'm going to be a good dad, a damn good one, just like my pops was for me.

The rest of the flight is uneventful, compared to feeling my babies move. I make it through the landing without hurling everywhere, and then we're finally able to exit.

When my feet hit the ground of the terminal, actual fucking land, I could almost kiss it.

The airport is busy, both incoming and outgoing traffic, so it takes us longer than anticipated to get our bags.

"Did you schedule an Uber or is your mom picking us up?" Em asks as we walk to the exit gate.

"Babe, there are no Ubers where we're going." I laugh, shaking my head. Emery knows I live on a farm, sure, but I don't think she realizes just how far outside of civilization we're going to be. It's a one stoplight, tiny grocery store and ten churches kind of town.

The nearest Target is at least an hour away.

"I doubt you're even going to have a signal way out here, and my ma's Wi-Fi is spotty... at best, so I'd go ahead and send whatever emails and texts you have to now."

Her eyes widen. "Graham! I have to be able to stay in contact with work," She begins furiously typing way on her phone. "Ugh, I didn't even think about it being an issue in my hurry to get everything ready."

"It's okay, I'll take you into town if you need to send anything and the internet isn't working. Told you I lived in a small town. Just wait."

I wheel both of our suitcases out the door while Em holds her pregnancy pillow and purse close to her. We finally make it outside the gate and onto the sidewalk.

The first thing I hear is a squeal, followed by, "Graham Anthony Adams!"

Emery and I both look over at my ma, who's standing next to the old pickup that was once my father's, then mine, and now is hers. She's an old Chevy, but man is she fine. Considered vintage, she's still in pristine condition. Her red paint unchipped, and the chrome of her mirror still shining like the day I left her. And Ma... she looks just the way I remember.

Short, cropped gray hair, a worn pair of blue jeans with a white shirt and her signature plaid button down over it.

Ma rushes over to me, her blue eyes that match mine filled with tears as she pulls me into her arms. Letting go of the suitcases, I wrap my arms around her and squeeze.

"God, baby, I've missed you so much," she breathes into my ear.

My heart squeezes with guilt. It has been way too long since I've been home, and I feel like an asshole for it.

She leans back, taking me in, shaking her head on a watery laugh. "How is it possible that you're even bigger since the last time you've been here? Wait till Allie sees you."

Speaking of my sister... "Where is Allie?"

"She was busy trying to get the house ready. She'll be waiting when we get back. Now, are you going to introduce me to this beautiful girl or just have her standin' here feeling awkward?"

I laugh and look over at Emery. Her cheeks are as pink as her shirt, and she looks so nervous that I reach out and slide my hand in hers, offering her the same kindness she offered me on the plane. Except I wish it was real.

"Ma, this is Emery Davidson. Em, this is my ma."

Emery extends her hand for my ma to shake, but Ma passes it up and pulls Emery in for one of her hugs. Emery just hugs her back and laughs as mom pulls back to look at her.

"Sorry, sweetheart, I need to take a good look at the woman who has my son so happy."

"He makes me very happy too, Mrs. Adams."

Ma shakes her head and waves her hand. "Call me Michelle, sweetheart. You're part of the family now! Graham, go on and get the bags loaded into the truck so we can head home. I made your favorite tonight, red beans and rice with sweet cornbread."

Oh god.

My stomach grumbles at the mention of it. Women should know, the way to a man's heart isn't actually through his dick, it's through his stomach.

"That sounds amazing," Emery says, "I can't remember the last time I had an actual home-cooked meal. I basically survive off of DoorDash."

"Well, honey, trust me, you'll never go hungry at my house. C'mon."

I do as Ma says and load our suitcases into the bed of the truck, along with Em's pregnancy pillow, and then open the door and help her into the cab of the truck.

I spend the entire drive out of the city and to the farm, pointing things out to Em, who watches enthusiastically. I'm surprised she isn't bored out of her mind, but if she is, she doesn't let on. She just nods and asks Ma and me both questions while we ride.

I show her where I got into my first car wreck when I hit a cow, yes, an actual cow, where I graduated high school, the place where my father's buried. I never realize how much I miss home until I'm here again. All the little places are ingrained in my soul, a part of the person I am today. I'll always be a small-town boy at heart.

After an hour's ride, we arrive at the farm, pulling through the gates with Adams etched in the iron of the gate, and Ma smiles at Emery. "Home sweet home."

She pulls the truck down the driveway, until the white farmhouse I grew up in comes into view, followed by the big red barn behind it.

All these years, and it still hasn't changed. Well, maybe it

THE SCORECARD

could use some paint on the shutters, which I make a note to do before I leave. There are a few missing shingles, and the hinges on the doors look like they're a little rusty, but it's nothing I can't fix while I'm here.

It's home. Always will be.

When I think of the future, when I'm retired from hockey, and living my life with my wife and kids, I think about living in a place just like this. Land for my kids to run after the dog on, a big house with a wraparound porch, so I can drink my beer and watch them play, and a big pond that ices over in the winter, so I can teach my babies to skate, and to shoot a puck just like my pop taught me. I never forgot those days, and to this day, the memories I made at this house live with me.

All I want is a family who loves me.

A life I'm proud of.

Ma puts the truck in park and hops out, walking up the lawn to greet my little sister Allie, who's leaning against one of the pillars of the porch with a smirk on her lips. She's taller, a little more filled out since I've last seen her, but she's got the same mischievous glint in her eyes.

"You ready?" I ask Em, looking over at her.

She nods. "I am. Your mom is the best, I see why you love her so much."

"Best woman I've ever known. She made me a good man. I owe everything to her."

I open the door and get out, the gravel of the dirt driveway crunching beneath my shoes. Emery gets out behind me and I shut the door, facing my sister.

"Well, well, look at what the cat's drug home," she taunts.

"You know what they say, you always come home." I grin and pick her up, spinning her around for a hug.

Growing up, Allie was my best friend. While I don't get to

see her as much as I'd like with me living in Chicago, and her life here, she's still that person for me.

It's why I understand and respect Emery and Reed's relationship as much as I do, because I get it.

"You asshole, you didn't bring me any deep dish?" Allie groans when I set her down on her feet.

"Language," Ma chides, pushing past us into the house.

"Can't exactly shove it in my carry-on, Allie." I turn toward Em and grab her hand, tugging her gently against my side. "Allie, this is Em. Em this is my little sister, Allie."

Allie smiles and gives her a quick hug. "Hi Emery. It's nice to meet the woman who's putting up with my brother. I feel for you, I do."

This makes Emery laugh, a real genuine one that has me smirking in response. "It's nice to meet you too. Your home is beautiful. Breathtaking and peaceful."

Allie nods, looking out beyond the porch. "Yeah, it's got charm that speaks for itself. Did you know my dad built it? He drew the plans himself and worked on it for over two years until it was complete."

I was always so proud to tell people that. That my dad had a dream, and he brought it to life with his bare hands. That's the kind of man he was, a man who wasn't afraid to dream, and believed that by working hard and never giving up, you'd watch those dreams come true.

It's kind of funny...my father who worked from sunup to sundown, devoting his life to blue collar work, with his head in the clouds.

I miss him. Every day and as my eyes slide over all the places on the farm that he touched, and built, and dreamed, the pain washes over me.

The once bright red barn, now worn with the years of age

and weather, sits behind the house, housing my dad's tractors and equipment. There are stalls for horses and goats, as well as the stray animals Allie would bring around at all hours of the night.

She was always like that, saving strays that wandered onto the farm.

Emery's eyebrows shoot up in shock. "Wow, I had no idea he was so talented. How incredible, and to have this special piece of him here with you. The details on the house..." She trails off, walking around and running her hand over the whitewashed wood of the porch rail.

Then she glances up at me, her blue eyes full of unshed tears. "I'm so sorry for your loss. He sounds like an incredible man. I'm sorry."

Her hand tightens in mine, squeezing. Those words hit me right in the chest.

Her compassion. Her empathy.

They're obvious at this moment, and it makes my heart pound against my rib cage violently.

Instead, I pull Emery to me and plant a long, lingering kiss on her lips, surprising her and Allie both. After a brief pause, she melts into my touch. Remembering that we're supposed to be engaged, she brings her hand up to my jaw then lets it rest there while I kiss her so hard, we're both breathless when she finally breaks the kiss.

Our gaze never breaks as something... new passes between us.

"Welp, that's my cue. Meet you two lovebirds inside," Allie says quietly, leaving us alone on the wraparound porch, both of us caught up in the moment.

"Graham..." she murmurs, bringing her hand up to her lips.

I step forward, sliding my hands up her jaw. "I know this

isn't real to you, but every single second I'm around you, it becomes real for me."

My eyes search hers, and I drop a quick kiss to her lips, then step back, grabbing her hand and wordlessly leading her inside.

I'll let her sit on my words.

Hopefully by the time this is over, she'll realize that I've been crazy about her from the start, and it won't be fake any longer.

It'll be real.

―――

Later that night, with Ma's famous red beans in front of us, we talk about everything I've missed since I've been in Chicago. Which is surprisingly a lot, since there's only a thousand people who live in our town.

I've been listening to Allie gossip with Ma and Emery about a book club that's formed in town, where they're apparently reading romance novels that are not for the faint of heart, but the entire time I've been so damn nervous to tell them the news, I haven't been able to sit still.

"She literally fainted on the floor. Clutched her imaginary pearls and slid right off the chair. I almost choked on my wine." Allie grins, taking another sip of her homemade wine. Another of Ma's specialties.

Emery laughs so hard; I can feel the table in front of us shake as her stomach sits against it.

For the trip, she wore a baggy shirt that covered the babies until tonight, when we were able to tell Ma and Allie the news.

"Oh my lord, stop it, Allie," Ma chides, hiding a smirk

behind her glass, "You brought a book that those old women have no business readin' and you know it."

Allie shrugs. "Alien erotica is in right now. Something about a guy with a big blue di-"

"*Allie Elizabeth!*"

I sputter over the mouthful of red beans, almost choking on it. Glancing at Emery, she's laughing so hard she's got tears streaming down her face.

What in the hell is happening?

"Can't a man enjoy his mama's cooking in peace? Shit Allie," I grumble.

"Sure, big bro"

The smirk on Allie's face tells me she doesn't give two shits whether or not I die on a plate of red beans.

Cruel woman.

"Well Ma, Allie Cat... Emery and I have something to tell you.

Emery looks up from her plate and over at me, then plasters on a blinding smile. So real, even I almost fall for it.

"Em's pregnant... With... twins," I say, reaching over and clasping my hand in hers.

"Oh my god," Allie says, her mouth agape.

"I know you're both probably shocked. But, we wanted to tell you in person, rather than over the phone. It was bad enough that we had to tell you about our engagement over the phone. We had to be here to tell you."

Ma's eyes are huge, and her jaw hangs open in surprise. It's like she's frozen in place. But then I see the tears welling in her eyes from across the table.

"Ma?"

Emery squeezes my hand in hers.

"I'- I'm going to be a grandmother?" she whispers, the tears in her eyes spilling over onto her cheeks. She brings her hand to her mouth as she begins to cry. "Babies? Two babies?"

We nod together.

"It's very rare since neither side has twins," Emery adds. "I brought some ultrasound pictures to show you both, if you'd like to see them?"

Sniffling, Ma nods her head. "Of course, I'd love to see them."

Emery stands, and I help her scoot her chair back. She walks over to stand between Allie and Ma and shows them the picture she had in her purse. Allie squeals when Emery points the babies out.

"This is baby A, and this is baby B. These are their feet," Emery says proudly, pointing her purple manicured nail at the small beans on the ultrasound picture.

"Oh God, even their little feet are so cute. I can't take it!" Ma clutches her heart, her words shaky as she leans in closer to get a better look.

"These are for you. For you to put on the fridge or wherever," Emery says, looking up at me.

Fuck, seeing her with Ma and Allie. I love it. Too much. Knowing that it's not real. It's like dangling a piece of fresh bread over a starving man, knowing that he'll never be able to have it, and he'll starve to death without it.

"Graham... you're going to be a daddy. My baby is going to have babies of his own."

Standing from my chair, I walk over and slide my arm around Ma's shoulders, clutching her close to me.

"Your daddy would be so proud of the man you're becoming, sweetheart. I hope you know that. He's watching you right now, and don't you forget it."

Her words cause the emotion in my chest to tighten. I

haven't cried in years, but right now, I feel hot tears sting my eyes.

I'd do anything to have another moment with him, for him to see me right now. I hope that I'm making him proud, and that I'm half the man he was.

"I'm going to be a kickass aunt," Allie says, hugging Emery. "Proud of you Graham Cracker."

I'm a grown man, and she's still calling me by my childhood nickname.

"Thanks, Allie Cat."

Emery smiles, watching the exchange between the two of us.

"Emery, now that you're unofficially officially part of the family, I need to tell you all about the embarrassing things I know about Graham. Did you know he used to pee the bed till he was ten?"

I stiffen. "What the hell, Allie?"

She smirks, tossing back the rest of her wine. "And he slept with a teddy bear until he moved out. Bet you he's still got it. What was it called, Graham?"

"I hate you," I grumble.

"Dr. Dickey! That was it!" Allie exclaims.

I literally hate my sister right now. Jesus fucking Christ.

Emery laughs. "You two remind me so much of Reed and me. Growing up, all we had was each other and our mom."

"Well, welcome to the family, Emery," Ma says. "We're so happy you're here. When are you due?"

"January. My doctor is monitoring my pregnancy closely, since twin pregnancies can be more high risk than normal pregnancies, but as of now, everything looks great. He did say that he doubts I will go full term, as most twin pregnancies don't.

But, we should be able to find out the sex at my next appointment."

Allie squeals. "I hope it's girls."

"Me too," Emery says, smiling, "but your brother wants boys. Go figure."

"Hey, gotta have someone to carry on the Adams' name."

"Oh, Emery, speaking of babies, I'll have to show you all of Graham's baby books while you are here and give you two a few pictures to take home. I wonder who the babies will favor more. Oh, I'm just so happy. Getting married and becoming a family. I'm so proud of you, Graham," Ma says, happiness shining in her eyes.

Sitting here surrounded by my family and Em, I feel happier than I have in months.

It feels like, for the first time, everything has fallen in place, except one missing piece.

Emery's heart.

EMERY

FIFTEEN

"RISE AND SHINE, BEAUTIFUL."

My eyes crack open, and I see Graham hovering over me, a wide grin on his too handsome face. The first thing I notice, aside from my baby daddy standing over me, is that it's still dark outside.

The alabaster white walls of his childhood bedroom are still blanketed by the pale moonlight, sitting low in the sky. I stretch my arms over my head, trying to shake the grogginess inside me.

I am not, and never will be, a morning person.

"What time is it?" I groan.

Graham looks down at his watch then back at me. "Four thirty."

"In the morning?"

My voice is a hoarse screech, much different than his way too perky, sunshine timbre for this early in the morning. The man has literally *lost* his mind.

"You do realize that the sun isn't even up yet?" I pull the warm duvet back over my head and close my eyes.

I don't actually expect an answer to my question, so when I

feel a tug at the covers, I groan for the second time in five minutes.

"Of course, I do. I wanna take you somewhere, come on."

Hearing the excitement in his voice is the only reason I begrudgingly toss off the covers and put my feet on the cold wood floor.

"Fine."

I've never been a morning person, and I do not foresee that changing in the near future. I'm wearing an old t-shirt with a pair of shorts, and before I can even get up to get dressed, Graham shakes his head.

"Nah, just wear this. We're not going far."

He extends his hand, holding out an old sweatshirt that I've seen him wear. I nimbly take it from him, and pull it over my head, relishing the fact that it smells exactly like he does. Warm, happy... him.

God, my hormones must be raging. That has to be the reason I'm currently sniffing his sweatshirt like a weirdo.

We've only been at his childhood home for four days and honestly? I love it more than I ever imagined I would. Granted, there isn't a "country" bone in my body, but there's something peaceful and serene about being cut off from the rest of the world.

The farm, his family, all of it. It's not what I expected, but in the best way. We've spent the past four days with his mom and sister, doing things on the farm and getting to know each other. I've learned how to muck a stall, which is not the best experience, but I did it without complaint because his mama was so proud when I finished it.

That's something I've quickly learned about his family: they're infectious. You *want* to make his mom smile, to impress her and earn her wide smile and loving eyes.

So, I'm officially a bona-fide country girl.

After I slip on my shoes, I follow quietly behind Graham as we exit the house and climb into the old truck that's parked out front.

Graham cranks it up, and we pull behind the house, past the barn, into the expanse of hills and fields that are spread out behind his property. There's only a gravel road that seems to wind around the property. It's still dark, the sprinkle of stars scattered across the sky, and the bright headlights of the truck shine out in front of us.

We ride in comfortable silence, partly because I'm still half asleep, but mostly because I'm enjoying the scenery of his home. It's nothing like Chicago, and surprisingly, the longer I'm here, the more and more it appeals to me.

After a short drive, he pulls up near a field that's full of… strawberries?

He opens my door and extends his hand to help me out.

"What is this?"

Instead of answering, he pulls out a blanket from behind me, and then reaches for my hand once more.

His warm, strong hand slides in mine and he clasps gently, tugging me right alongside him. We climb the steep hill just in front of us until we're at the very top.

I suck in a breath when I see the expanse in front of me.

From this very spot, basked in the pale moonlight, you can see for miles, the hilly farming land with cattle, and horses running wild in the fields. There are rows of fruit, and trees of apples. Even blanketed in inky darkness, it looks like something from a painting.

The stars above shine brighter than I've ever seen. In the city, the skies are full of skyscrapers, and smog, making it nearly impossible to see anything beyond the lights of the city. Truthfully, I've never seen a sky so calm and still before.

"Wow," I breathe, my eyes still taking in everything in front of me.

Graham laughs low and hoarse as he spreads out the blanket he grabbed from the truck. He takes my hand and helps me sit next to him, like holding my hand is the most natural thing in the world to him.

So close that our shoulders brush together, and I breathe in his rugged yet calming scent.

"When I was little, my pops and I, we'd always be the first ones up. Before the sun rose every day, we'd be up and having breakfast, getting ready to do everything that needed to be done on the farm." Resting his arms around his legs, he gazes out in front of him. "Man, I'd grumble and moan about it. Well, at first, I did. Then I realized that it was time I would get to spend uninterrupted with my pops. He... He was my best friend."

His voice cracks with pain, and I reach out to lace my fingers between his, squeezing gently. I don't like the sadness etched into his features. I wish with all my heart that I could take it away and bring back the smile that I've come to like far too much.

Clearing his throat of emotion, he continues, "It was my time with him, just mine. I look back now, and I'd give anything for just five more minutes of those mornings. You never know how important a moment is, until it passes you by and you can't get it back." Hearing the raw pain in his voice does something to my insides, makes me ache to put my arms around him.

"Anyway, those mornings I'd follow him around, watching everything he did, and trying to do it myself. But no matter where we were, he'd find a way to be right here on this very hill to see the sunrise. Every Saturday. We'd be here. And he'd say to me, 'Son, never stop living like it's your last day.' I live by that. I think that's why everyone calls me Sunshine, because I'm rarely in a bad mood, I rarely let shit get to me because I took that advice to heart from my pops. If I wake up tomorrow and the world around me ends, I want to be satisfied with the man I was and the life I lived."

He finally looks over at me, raw emotion glistening in his eyes. "That's all I want out of life. Not the money or the fame. Not the brand deals. Hell, all of it could disappear tomorrow and I'd use the money I made to take care of my family. My babies, my ma, my sister... you."

My stomach flips. "Graham, I don't need th-"

He stops me before I can finish. "I know you don't, and that's something that I fucking love about you, Em, the fact that you don't *need* anyone. You're independent, you've got the entire world in the palm of your hand. It's not that I don't think you can provide for yourself, or that you want me to buy you material things. It's that *I* want to. I want to be a man that our babies are proud of. I wanna be just like my father, and I want to be half the man that he used to be."

Emotion claws its way up my throat and hits me in an unexpected wave.

"He would be proud, Graham, of who you are. Tell me more about him. About what he was like. Tell me all of the things, so I can love him the way you do."

Graham holds my gaze for a moment, his throat bobbing as he swallows. "He was kind. He'd give the shirt off his back for anyone. People in town would call him for help on their cars, or their house, and he'd drop whatever he was doing and go. Always put everyone before himself. I wish that I had more time with him." He pauses, looking down at my hand in his, then back up at me. "I wish he could've met you. Met my children. I'll keep his memory alive, like I always have. By being the kind of dad he was. Patient, compassionate, protective."

For the first time, I *see* Graham Adams.

Not the Graham I *thought* I knew or the Graham that the media perceives him to be. The guy who can't commit or settle down, whose biggest responsibility is on the ice, and outside of that, nothing else.

I see someone who would do anything for his family, a guy that loves his friends and is fiercely loyal. Honest to a fault, ferociously protective of those that he loves. Those are the things that I've learned about Graham in the past few weeks. I've seen the way he treats his mom, or lets his sister call him his childhood nicknames, how even though he's exhausted he still does anything and everything they need help with at the farm.

"The point of all that was that I just wanted to bring you out here. So you could experience it. So I could give you a little piece of me. Of my family. Of my dad."

He looks away, then back out in front of him. In the midst of the deep conversation, I hadn't realized that the sun was beginning to rise. A vast, deep orange that seemed to settle around us like a cloak.

It's breathtaking. The most beautiful, tranquil thing I've ever experienced alongside a man I thought I knew, but I'm learning that I didn't really know at all.

That I may have judged him all wrong.

And knowing he's not what I thought... that isn't good for my heart. I can protect it from a man who isn't worthy, but from someone who is pure and good down to the marrow of his bones?

Well, let's just say I didn't plan for that and that's what scares me most of all.

GRAHAM

SIXTEEN

A WEEK into visiting my ma and sister, I realized *just* how fucked I am.

And not because my sister and Ma have spent every waking moment with Emery, but because every moment *I* spend with Emery Davidson, I realize how hard I'm falling.

It's like the ground has opened up beneath my feet, and I'm free-falling. For this girl with the bunny slippers. For my best friend's little sister. For the mother of my babies.

For a girl who will probably never let me close enough to penetrate the wall she's built up around her heart.

"Why are there so many different stroller choices?" Emery groans, dropping her head onto the magazine of strollers she's been idly flipping through for the last hour.

"Mmm. Not sure, babe."

She points out two strollers that look exactly the fucking same. I mean... seriously, I can't tell a single difference between them, aside from one saying Elite, and the other not.

My brow furrows in confusion.

What the hell is happening right now?

They look *exactly* the fucking same.

"Uh... those are the same?" I say.

This is not my area of expertise and, apparently, not Em's either, judging by her reaction.

Emery groans again then slams the magazine closed and leans back in the chair, her hand going to her stomach. "I want food. Like, horribly bad for me food that is full of sugar or grease. Maybe both. And I want to never have to choose between strollers and car seats, and baby wearers. Or breast pumps or any of this stuff that I know nothing about. I've been looking at statistics and car-seat reports, and all of these different choices for so long, my eyes are going to fall out of my head."

"Whenever we get home, we'll go to the store and talk to someone. They have to know more about this stuff than us. Plus, you could talk to Maddison or Juliet; they've been here before and probably have tons of shit to tell you about."

"True. I'm going to call Maddison whenever we get home. Oh!" She shoots up from her chair and comes back with her laptop, taking her seat again.

"Our gender ultrasound is scheduled for the Tuesday we get back."

Finally. Fuck, I feel like it's been ten years since we found out she was pregnant. Not true, I know, but it feels like it. I've heard of my friends' wives waiting to find out the sex of their baby until birth, and I am so fucking thankful that Em isn't torturing me that way.

I need to know if my gut is right.

Girls.

My eyes drift back to the magazine, and I shrug. "I can't help with all of this, even though I wish I could, but I think I can help with the food part. You wanna go somewhere with me?"

A grin tugs at the corner of her lips. "Another sunrise?"

I shake my head. "Nah, how about a sunset and something better?"

She pauses briefly, glancing back down at the magazine spread out in front of her. "I need a break, so I'm down."

Best thing I've heard all day.

After a quick shower, I wait for Em on the porch with Ma talking about the babies, and hell was it well worth it when Emery comes through the screen door, stepping out onto the porch.

She's wearing my favorite pair of cut off shorts, with a fitted tank that hugs her stomach. Her hair is wet and tied to the side in a messy braid. Lip gloss shines on her plump lips.

So goddamn kissable.

I shoot up from the rocking chair and walk over to her, sliding my hands up her jaw before she can protest, and I fucking kiss her.

The lip gloss on her lips tastes like cherries, and fuck, if we were alone, I'd do a lot more than kiss it clean off her lips. It's been seven days since I've been inside her and I'm losing my damn mind.

"Graham," she breathes, holding onto my hand for support.

I grin.

"Sorry babe."

"You two... you remind me so much of your father and me. Young and crazy in love. Couldn't keep our hands off each other if we tried. I love seeing you happy," Ma says softly, observing us from her rocker with a smile on her face.

It hits me somewhere deep in my stomach, a nagging

feeling and a reminder that this is fake at least... to Emery it is... and how much I wish it wasn't.

"Thanks Ma. We'll be back, but don't wait up, okay?"

She laughs. "You say that like you aren't a grown man. Bye you two. Have fun."

I lace my fingers with Emery's and lead her to the truck, helping her inside, then walk around to climb in the cab beside her. I pull the truck out onto the highway in the direction of town, and Emery's face lights up.

"Where are we going?"

"You'll see." I smirk, turning the old radio up some. She watches out the window the entire ride, and I watch her.

Like a moth to a flame, I can't stop my eyes from drifting to her as the old truck bumps along the highway. Part of me wants to pull over, just to sink inside her, and watch those plump lips as she cries my name. The other just wants to wrap my arms around her and hold her.

A feeling I don't think I've ever felt when it came to a woman.

The ride passes quickly, and before I realize it, I'm pulling into the Baptist church parking lot on the outside of town, now lit up by the Seventy Second Annual Strawberry Festival.

I look over at Em. Her eyes are wide, the lights of the fair reflecting on her baby blues.

She looks over at me excitedly. "Oh my god. Is that a *Ferris wheel*?"

"Sure is. This is the Seventy Second Annual Strawberry Festival. We do it every year. Rides, a pie-eating contest, a jam-making contest, lots of greasy food, games. Oh, and a dunking booth."

I don't think I've ever seen Emery so excited, and fuck, it makes me happy.

THE SCORECARD

Laughing, I get out, walk around the truck and open her door.

She scrambles from the car breathlessly. "I've never been to a fair like this. Can you believe that? We went to Six Flags when I was like four, but that's it, and I hardly remember it. Oh god, I can *smell* the greasy goodness."

She all but moans the last part, and I can't stop the laugh from tumbling from my lips.

Tossing my arm over her shoulder, I pull her against me and we walk to the entrance, where I pay for our tickets and then we're ushered through by the attendant.

"Hope you like strawberries." I laugh, nodding to the assortment of strawberry well... everything.

Her grin widens, and she looks up at me. "I happen to love strawberries. But, first, food. Greasy, lots of fat goodness. Mmmm."

I know exactly what to get her.

We make our way to the concession stand and get in line. Her eyes go wide when she sees the things listed on the menu.

"Oh my god. Fried Oreos? What is this gloriousness?" I can practically see her drooling from here.

"Good as fuck. But I'm a fan of funnel cake. There's nothing better."

She scans the menu in front of her again and chews on her lip in deliberation, like it's the hardest thing she's ever had to decide.

"How about we order it all?" I laugh.

Her eyes dart to mine. "Don't tempt me, Adams. I'm eating for three."

We finally make it to the front of the line, and then I proceed to order half the shit on the menu, laughing when the teenager working the register's eyes go wide.

I shrug, pulling out my wallet. "My girl can eat."

That earns me an elbow to the side. Hell, I'd probably get a damn hard-on to see her eat all of this.

I don't know why women are so worried about eating in front of a man. Because for me...There's nothing sexier than seeing my girl eat.

Nothing.

I want her to fuel her body, especially when there's a good chance after this, we'll get back home and I'll work her out. Extensively.

Em and I sit at a picnic table on the side of the concession stand, and she looks around with excitement, hardly able to sit still in her seat.

"I know I can't ride any rides, but I think the Ferris wheel would be okay," she contemplates.

"Yep, I emailed Dr. Brown about it. He said it's okay."

"You checked with my doctor?"

I nod. "Of course. I wouldn't do anything that wasn't safe for you or the babies, Em."

She opens her mouth to say something, but they call our number at the stand, signaling our order is ready.

"Hold that thought," I tell her, a wide smile on my face, before walking over to get the ridiculous amount of stuff we ordered in my arms then placing it in front of her.

She picks the funnel cake first, and when she takes her first bite, her eyes roll back in her head as she lets out a moan around the mouthful of powdered covered cake.

Fuck, first it was ice cream, now it's funnel cake.

My dick hasn't gotten the memo when it involves Emery and food.

"Oh my god. This is literal heaven. Like an angel actually came down and hand delivered this to a carnival carney. I'm convinced. Mmm." Shoveling another bite into her mouth, she moans again.

"Satisfies the greasy and the full of sugar in one go, huh?"

She nods. "Perfection. Next up, an actual fried Oreo."

We spend the next thirty minutes sampling everything in front of us, and ultimately, it's no surprise that the funnel cake wins.

It's been my favorite since I was a kid. I quickly toss the leftover food away, and then we make our way to the games.

"No, we should probably skip the games. I would hate to beat you after you just gave me that delicious food." She snickers, crossing her arms.

"Is that a... challenge, Davidson?" My eyebrow raises in question. "Sure you wanna go there?"

"You tell me. I'm always up for a challenge, are you?"

Fuck, this crazy girl, I'm done for.

"Put your money where your mouth is, babe. Loser signs up for the dunk tank. No take backs," I tell her, pointing to the dunking booth full of water across the courtyard. She looks over at it, then back at me, and steels her jaw.

"Prepare to get wet."

I smirk. "Nah, that'll be you. Now... and later."

"Pig," she retorts.

"You love it."

Three rounds of darts and balloons later, I got my ass kicked by my baby mama, and that's how I ended up in the damn tank, waiting to get dunked.

That's the last time I ever underestimate all four-foot-eleven of her.

"Maybe next time you make a bet with me, you'll consider the outcome." The smug grin hangs on her lips. Even with the crowd surrounding us, and the more than good chance that I'm about to get my ass soaking wet, I still want to kiss that mouth, attitude and all.

Actually, it's my favorite thing about her.

That mouth.

I shrug, my smirk only growing wider. "I will admit that I didn't expect to find myself here, but I'll take you on any day, Davidson."

I clap my hands together and open my arms wide. "Gimme your best shot, babe."

Emery squares her shoulder, then rears back and throws the bright yellow ball at the target, narrowly missing.

My ass clenches as it slams against the outer ring of the target.

Thank fuck.

"Yesssss," I yell, laughing when she sticks her tongue out at me. God, I'm crazy about this girl.

Emery looks at me with pure determination in her eye and prepares to throw the next ball.

I should've known better than to celebrate after the first miss, because the second time, she doesn't.

She nails it square on the target, the dunking booth siren goes off and the board my ass is on falls out from beneath me, plunging me into the water below.

My feet hit the ground and I push upwards, slinging the water from my hair and face before pulling myself out.

"Holy shit." Emery pants through tears of laughter. She's laughing so hard, her entire body shakes as she doubles over. "Oh God, this is the best thing I've ever seen. Graham Adams literally eating his words."

I'm fucking soaked, head to toe, even my shoes are squishing with each step I take toward Emery. Before she can stop me, I wrap my arms around her and spin her around.

"Graham, stop, stop! I'm getting wet!"

Growling, I lean closer until my lips brush against the shell of her ear and whisper, "How about we skip the Ferris wheel so I can eat your pussy under the stars."

Her body goes tight in my arms, and she stops thrashing. She looks up at me, her eyes wide and full of desire, before shuddering lightly. "Graham." She breathes my name. It's low and hoarse, like my words have as much effect on her as they do me.

"Nah, I'm not letting you skip the Ferris wheel. After, we'll go to my spot, and I promise to make you come on my face."

I smirk when her cheeks turn red under the fair lights. I lift my shirt, ringing out the excess water from the fabric, and her eyes drift to my stomach, and when they do, a carnal look passes over her face.

"Later," I mumble against her ear and lace my fingers with hers.

The past week has changed something between us. Emery's... different. It's like whatever was holding her back has weakened, and if anything, we've become actual friends. Spending the week away from everyone and everything has made her open up. Both of us are exploring sides of each other we haven't until now. We've talked about our families, laughed harder than I have in months, talked about the future for our babies.

Hell, she's only done the minimum for work, putting it aside to spend time with my family and get to know them.

It feels different, better.

I can feel it tonight, more than ever, and fuck, I just want to hold on to it. Prove to her that this isn't fake between us, prove that what we're both feeling is real, and I could actually make her happy for the long haul.

I know that it won't be easy, but I'm not going to give up. That's not who I am.

Once we get to the Ferris wheel, I hand the attendant our tickets, and he puts us in a red car on the ride. Emery slides in beside me excitedly, ready for the ride to begin.

"This is incredible, Graham. Thank you. For everything."

"It's nothing, Em."

She shakes her head, her stormy eyes holding mine just as the ride lurches forward. "No, it's... it's everything. I just feel like I know the real you now. Not the man I thought I had figured out from the start."

Side by side, the Ferris wheel takes us higher, high above the fair, and the people scurrying around below us. So high it feels like I could reach out and touch the clouds.

"You hated me, Emery. You can just say that." I laugh, trying to lighten my tone, because they sounded harsher than intended. "You're nothing like I thought either, but I always thought you were gorgeous, and I would've given my left nut to date you. But you clearly hated the ground I walked on. What happened to make you dislike me?"

Her gaze averts, out to the darkened sky around us, a mask of hurt etched on her features.

But why?

"I-... I overheard you and Briggs. That night at Reed's."

My brow furrows. Which night? Huh?

She must see the confusion on my face because she continues, "The night that I was housesitting for Reed and Holland. You and Briggs stumbled in, and I almost decapitated you both with the hockey stick."

Oh, *fuck*. I was plastered that night. I don't even remember how we made it to Reed's. I was a rookie, doing whatever I could to fit in, to make a name for myself in the NHL, and

Briggs had called and wanted to get shit faced. He was dealing with a lot of shit, so I agreed. The rest is hazy. I vaguely remember Emery answering the door in a t-shirt. A tiny fucking t-shirt. The same tiny t-shirt I came to, more than once.

"I was really drunk that night, Em. If I did anything or said anything..." I trail off, shaking my head.

"You did. Say something." She looks back at me. "I overheard you telling Briggs that you wouldn't touch me if your life depended on it."

My mind begins to spin, trying to recall the conversation, anything from that night, and I come up blank.

Before I can even speak, she continues.

"I mean, I wasn't even interested in you, Graham, but your words... they had power. Power I never realized I even gave to anyone else. You said it would be like sleeping with Reed, and that you didn't like my independent attitude."

With every word, the knot in my stomach tightens. Fuck, she's felt like this for so long and I had no idea. The mother of my kids thought I was... disgusted by her.

Fuck.

"I'm so sorry, Emery... I..." I clench my jaw. Fucking idiot. Reaching out, I take her hand in mine. "I'm so fucking sorry. I'm an asshole. Shit, I was so drunk that night, I honestly don't even remember saying any of that. It wasn't true, and I wish I could take it back."

"The next day you flirted with me after you said all of those things behind my back. I figured you were exactly what everyone said you were: a player who didn't care about the women he slept with. And I don't like players. I'm done being played. I've got my own shit, my own baggage, and that's why your words hurt. It reminded me that people always show who they truly are, and that honesty is never something you should have to settle for. It reminded me of the last man who was dishonest with me, and why I don't trust relationships. So, in any relationship, Graham, I value honesty above all else, and you need to know that. That's why I'm putting all of my cards on the table and telling you how I feel now. I expect honesty, and it's only fair that I give it to you. I've been bottling this up, and now feels like the right time to put it all out..."

I officially feel like the biggest asshole on the planet.

"I know, Em. I'm sorry. Thank you for being honest with me. Truthfully, Briggs was probably interested in you, and I said stupid shit to try and deter him. Briggs was fucked up back then, out of control because of the shit going on with him, and I wouldn't have let him touch you over my dead body. If you didn't know, I've always had a thing for you."

She sucks in a sharp breath, a quiet one that I almost didn't catch. Her gaze holds mine, and she never lets go of my hand.

"I wasn't lying when I said that I saw you in the stands, and it was like you were the only person in the room. You took my breath away."

"Graham..." she says, trailing off. There's an edge to her voice, one that makes me swallow down the words I was about to say.

"I know, you want to be friends. I respect you and your decision. But I'm also not going to give up, Emery. I want you, and I want this, and I want to be very clear about that. What I feel for you is real, and it's not just because you're the mother of my kids, Em. It's because I've always been drawn to you, and now that I know you, I want you even more."

Her eyes shine with unshed tears as we go higher and higher on the Ferris wheel, the colorful lights reflecting in the watery tears. Angled toward me, I can't help but want to pull her closer.

I hate to see her cry, and even more now that I was the one to fucking cause it.

"Don't cry, Em." I reach up with my thumb to dry the tear that's slipped free.

"It's my stupid hormones. I can't stop crying. I cried this morning in the shower because I saw a *bird* outside the window. A bird, Adams."

I laugh. "You're fucking adorable when you cry."

She laughs, wiping the tears away.

"Friends?"

She nods. "Friends."

"Friends who make each other come." I throw in for good measure, because while I don't agree with *friends*, I'm not going to stop trying to make her fall in love with me.

"You're ridiculous," she says, rolling her eyes.

"Still the truth."

The smirk she gives me says everything I need to know.

GRAHAM

SEVENTEEN

I'M GOING out of my mind. A man is only so strong, and I could be the strongest man in the world and I *still* wouldn't stand a chance resisting Emery Davidson.

Not a fucking chance.

Emery Davidson is the kind of woman who brings men to their knees. Good thing being on my knees between my wife-to-be's thighs is *exactly* where I intend to stay.

I want nothing more than to drive her over the edge with my tongue and my cock, each and every chance I get.

Doesn't help that we're sleeping in the room where I grew up, sharing my childhood bed that barely fit me as a teenager, let alone a grown-ass man. Every morning for the last week, I've woken up with her ass pressed against my cock and had to use every ounce of willpower I had to pull myself out of bed and sprint to the bathroom to take care of it.

My hand isn't cutting it anymore, not when the girl of every wet dream I've had for the last two years is lying next to me.

Another breathy moan leaves her, and I roll over, shoving the pillow under my head to try and get comfortable.

Which doesn't work.

When I feel her ass brush against me, I groan.

"Em, I can't fucking take it anymore. I can't do it."

I hear her laugh, then she rolls over carefully, tucking her hands beneath her head as she gazes at me. The blue of her irises seems to burn brighter than normal, under the pale moonlight streaming in.

"What do you mean?" She bats her eyelashes, feigning innocence.

This girl.

Reaching out, I haul her against me, as gently as I can with her growing stomach. Gotta protect my girls.

"You know exactly what you're doing. Cruel woman. My dick's about to bust through my shorts," I complain, thrusting against her, so she can feel the evidence herself.

"Mmm, weren't you the one who said we should be hands-off while at your mom's house."

She whispers, snaking her hand down the front of my gym shorts, wrapping her fist around the length of me and squeezing... not even remotely gently.

I hiss in response. "Emery..."

A warning. My restraint is hanging by a damn thread and I'm about two seconds from fucking the shit out of her right in this bed.

"Graham," she breathes my name like a prayer, pumping me once, then again, "I need it. I need you to make it all better."

God damnit.

Fuck it.

I crash my lips to hers, drinking her in after depriving us both for the last week, savoring the sweetness of her kiss. My hands thread in her hair, holding her to me, angling her mouth so I can kiss her deeper, our tongues tangling in the hottest kiss of my life.

I tear my lips from hers, panting. "Can you be quiet? If I make it all better, will you be a good girl and be quiet?"

She nods, sucking her bottom lip into her mouth, causing me to kiss her once more, harder this time. Rougher than I usually am, but fuck, we've been all but edging each other for the last week. A brush against my cock, her ass grinding against me all night while she prances around in those cutoff jeans, made just for me to have to bite my fist to keep from taking her against every surface.

When I say I can't get enough of her, I mean it. I could have her every day and it still never be enough.

My fingers skim beneath the waistband of the old boxers of mine she threw on to go to sleep, and wordlessly pull them down her hips. Underneath, she's got on a pair of cheeky boy shorts that cause me to groan. I slide my hands beneath her and grab a fistful of her ass, leaning down to drag my nose along the seam of her pussy through the lace.

"I'll never get enough of this." I pull the underwear down her hips, slowly, carefully, even though the last thing I feel is patient. Dragging them down her legs, I remove them, leaving her bare.

Her skin is milky in the pale moonlight, kissed by the darkness, and I can't help but drag my tongue along the soft flesh of her inner thigh. I spread her open, admiring how perfect her pussy is, pink and glistening, waiting to be devoured.

I can say without a fucking doubt, I am a pussy guy. There is nothing I love more than eating my girl, every single day, tasting her, having her come on my face.

Tonight, though, I pull back and sit Emery up, then reach for the hem of my old high school t-shirt and haul it over her head. She sits in front of me, completely naked. Her tits heavier than when I first saw them, fuller and rounder. So fucking perfect.

I drop my lips to her nipple and tug it into my mouth, rolling it between my teeth as I suck.

Her moan echoes across the walls, causing me to pull back and shake my head, shushing her.

"If you can't be a good girl, baby, I can't let you come."

I grin smugly, and she narrows her eyes. I sit on the bed beside her and drag her on top of me, then scoot us to the headboard.

"I want you to ride my face, Emery," I whisper hoarsely.

Above me, her eyes go wide, and she tries to protest, but I stop her.

"Grab the headboard and ride me, baby."

Hesitation flits in her eyes. "Graham... No. I'm four times my normal size."

Pulling her closer, I slide my hands along her jaw, my eyes holding hers. "Not true. You're sexier than I've ever fucking seen you, and I want you to come on my face. We'll go slow, if that's what you want. But I love the taste of your pussy, and I want you to sit on my face."

I can still feel her reluctancy, but she lets me gently pull her above my head, positioning her directly above my face.

"Hands on the headboard, baby," I whisper softly.

For once, she doesn't argue and follows my direction, gripping the headboard.

"That's it, now let me taste you."

My hands grip her hips, pulling her down onto my mouth. My tongue flattens against her clit, settling her pussy on my face as she moans.

I let go of her hips to slide my finger inside her wet heat, groaning against the slick flesh.

Fuck, she's dripping.

We quickly find a rhythm, me languidly fucking her with my fingers while I suck her clit, scraping my teeth along the sensitive flesh, causing her to shiver above me. Her hips writhe against my mouth as she rides my face. Shamelessly, she chases the orgasm that soon has her hips locking, her hands flying to my hair as she bears her full weight onto me and trembles above me.

She comes with so much force, her back arches, and she almost loses her balance. My hands find her hips, steadying her as she rides out the wave of her orgasm, shuddering above me.

"That's my girl," I praise, savoring the taste of her on my tongue.

Once her hips have stopped moving and she's a pliant, panting mess above me, I gently flip her onto her hands and knees, careful of her stomach, propping her up with the pillows on the bed. I climb onto the bed behind her, quickly shedding my gym shorts and shirt, tossing them to the side.

My hands grip her hips gently, pulling her back slightly before grasping handfuls of her luscious ass, all but groaning as she opens up for me, revealing the wetness coating her inner thighs from where my mouth just was.

Leaning down, I trail kisses from her spine, slowly up to the blades of her shoulder.

She's fucking beautiful, so beautiful I can't wait another damn second to be inside her because, I'm convinced… Emery was made for me. And only me.

Slowly, I slide inside her, sinking inch by inch, until I don't know where I end and she begins. Unlike the frenzy I felt when I stripped her bare, now all I feel is the overwhelming need to take my time with her, worshiping every inch of her until every doubt she has in her head is gone.

My hips move, dragging in and out of her in lazy, unhurried thrusts. It's not enough, I can't get close enough to her in this position.

Reaching beneath us, my thumb strokes her clit, circling in rough movements as I fuck her.

"Graham." She moans quietly, her hands fisting into the bed.

Careful not to jostle her belly in any way, I pull out of her and lie on my side, taking her with me. Her back tightly to my front, both of us on our sides, as I grip her thigh and open her legs, sliding inside her from behind.

We each groan at the angle. I can't believe it's fucking possible to feel closer, to feel this good. One hand grips her thigh, hooking it back around my hip, the other grasping the back of her neck so I can kiss her.

This position is intimate. It's raw. It's the first time in my life I've felt connected to another person, body and soul.

When Emery's orgasm rocks her only seconds later, she takes me with her, tumbling somewhere we've never been. An unknown that I don't think I'll ever recover from.

Not when I know what it's like to have her this way.

There's no going back.

The next morning, I sleep in way past the sunrise after three rounds of the most intense sex of my life, and when I wake, Emery's gone. Her side of the bed is cold, meaning she's been gone for a while.

Hell, is she running scared after last night? I can't be the only one that felt it.

I slide out of bed and quickly throw on some clothes, following the scent of bacon into the kitchen. Before I even round the corner, I hear them. Ma whispering, and Emery laughing. When I walk in, they're standing at the kitchen island, both of them covered in flour. The smile on Emery's face causes my heart to fucking stop in my chest.

God, what a fucking sight.

Emery's wearing my grandma's apron, stained and worn, tied around her neck and protruding belly. Her hair is tied out of her face, but she's somehow gotten flour in it.

Ma grins, her blue eyes twinkling with amusement. "Morning sleepyhead."

"Good morning," I say gruffly, emotion suddenly clogging my throat.

"Good morning, handsome." Emery smirks, stirring a bowl of... something.

Clearing my throat, I ask, "What are you two making this early?"

Emery looks at Ma, then back at me, smiling widely. "We're making your Grandma Adams' famous pancakes. And yes, with the strawberries."

My stomach growls on cue. My grandma's pancakes are my favorite food in the world, and now Em's making them?

"She's learning, so she can make them for the babies and you when you get back home," Ma adds, rubbing Emery's arm lovingly. "You know, your grandma's secret was a drop of almond extract. She always said it gives them something she knew they were missing."

Emery looks completely at ease as she moves around Ma's kitchen, following her instructions on how to make gram's world-famous pancakes.

I take a seat at the kitchen table and just watch.

Watch them flit around the kitchen, laughing and talking about baby stuff.

"Have you and Graham decided on a color for the babies' room or are you waiting until you find out the gender?" Ma asks.

Emery looks over at me, her eyes slightly wide before she fumbles with the spoon she's holding. "Uh, we're still discussing all of those things. There's just so much to decide on. We don't want to make any quick decisions."

Ma nods. "I completely understand. There are a lot of big decisions that go into parenting. I wish there was a manual I could give you both to make life easier, but that's all a part of being parents. Learning as you go. You'll never be perfect at it, but what matters is that you learn from the mistakes you make and move forward. Being a mama can be hard, just as much as it is rewarding."

"When I first found out... about the pregnancy, I was scared. I never really expected to start a family, and suddenly, it was like I was either going to sink or swim. I realized in those weeks that maybe the unexpected was exactly what I needed to push me out of this comfort zone I had put myself in unintentionally. Throwing myself into my career, but putting a wall up to everything else," Emery says, looking over at me. "I'd like to think it was the babies guiding me to exactly where I was meant to be."

With me.

Exactly where she was meant to be.

Her unspoken words settle between us, and now more than ever, I have no doubt that we're exactly where we should be.

Each day, closer and closer to making her mine.

For real, and not for fake.

EMERY

EIGHTEEN

"THIS PICTURE here is when Graham was about two or so, and he had this obsession with being naked. I mean, buck naked, and constantly wanting to run around the yard, wearing nothing but a pair of old rubber boots his dad had found in the barn. I couldn't keep clothes on that boy to save my life." Michelle points to the picture of a naked Graham, playing in what looks like a round tin tub.

Just like she said, he's turned away from the camera, wearing a pair of yellow rubber boots and a black cowboy hat with nothing else. He has two little dimples right above his little butt cheeks.

I'm laughing so hard, tears stream down my face as I clutch my hand to my stomach. Michelle and I have been on the porch swing, side by side for the last hour, flipping through old family albums. It seems like she's kept a photo from every memory of their life, and I love it. I love seeing Graham as a child, seeing his father.

Although, he's fixing the fence only a few feet in front of us, shirtless with sweat gleaming down his ridiculously muscled back, and it's been very hard not to keep sneaking glances. My eyes drag down the flat, ribbed expanse of his stomach, as he picks up board after board and hammers it together. Each muscle rippling with the effect.

One last project before Michelle drops us off at the airport, and home we go. Back to reality.

Part of me isn't ready to leave this bubble that we've been in for the past two weeks. And an even bigger part of me isn't ready to leave Michelle and Allie behind.

"This is the oak tree, right over there, that Mark and I got married under when we were about the same age as you two." She runs her finger over the photo, as if she can feel him still here with us, and maybe she can. I'd like to hope that they can still feel his presence here with them. "I was three months pregnant with Graham here. He was a surprise, but we loved him from the second we knew. Something about your first baby always has a special place in your heart, meant just for them. He taught me how to be a mama."

"You've raised an amazing son, Michelle. He's a good man."

She nods. "A lot like his dad in lots of ways. He's hard on the exterior, but the boy is soft as pie on the inside. And I see the way he looks at you."

A sly smile sits on her lips. "Like you hung the moon. You're good for him. I can tell you keep him on his toes, and he needs a challenge. Nothing worth having comes easily."

If she only knew the truth. Guilt gnaws inside me, causing an open wound. I hate lying, now more than ever.

"I've been thinking." She glances back down at the photo of her and Mark under the tree, locked in a kiss. "If you and Graham wanted, you could get married here. Right under the oak tree where his father and I got married."

She points to the oak tree across the field, its massive limbs spreading out around the trunk, offering shade in the midst of blinding sunlight. The pure adoration in her eyes, the hopefulness and longing for what used to be makes my heart ache.

It's a beautiful idea, and it immediately makes me feel horrible.

Oh god, what do I even say?

I clear my throat. "I think Graham would like that."

"It's no pressure. I just wanted to offer it to you both. We'd be happy to accommodate your family and help with anything that you'll need. I can keep the babies while you two enjoy a honeymoon. Or in this case a baby moon." She smiles warmly, and the guilt in my stomach feels as heavy as lead.

"I'd like to talk to him about it, and let you know. If that's okay?"

"Of course, sweetheart." She flips another page. "Oh, this is one of my favorite photos."

It's a photo of all four of them together. Graham looks to be around four or five, wrapped up in his father's arms while his dad stands next to Michelle with Allie in hers. Their smiles are infectious. Just looking at the photo, I can feel the love. Feel how happy and content they were together.

It makes me think of Graham, the babies and me. What would our future look like? Would we have the same happiness as two separate families? Would our kids feel as loved as he did growing up? Now more than ever, my head is full of doubt. I felt the shift that night. When we stayed up until early in the morning, not able to get enough of each other. It wasn't sex.

It was more.

This is starting to feel like more, and it scares me. No, it downright *terrifies* me. I'm scared of being hurt. Of being betrayed. Of letting someone in, just to end up destroyed.

"I'm so sad that y'all are leavin' tomorrow," Michelle says.

A frown tugs at her lips just as Graham walks up the stairs of the porch, and flops down into the rocker across from us. He's drenched in sweat, and his cheeks have turned red from the hot sun.

"Me too Ma, but I'm sure once the babies are here you and Allie can come down and visit for a bit?"

She nods, "Of course. I can't believe you're going to be a daddy, Graham. I'm so proud."

"I had the best role models in the world Ma," He grins. I'm convinced he's the most charming man alive. Now I know why, more than ever, why girls lose their mind for those dimples.

I'm going to miss Michelle and Allie both, and I've only known them for a couple of weeks. But, in those couple of weeks, they've welcomed me with open arms, and I've enjoyed every moment spent here on the farm with them. Allie reminds me a lot of myself, and her company is easy, and something tells me that my mom and Michelle would love each other.

"I promise, I won't let Graham go so long without us coming to visit. I love this place, and I've loved getting to know you both. I wish we didn't have to go either." I tell her.

Michelle puts her arm over my shoulder and pulls me to her in a hug. Her hand rubs my arm lovingly.

"You know... I always said I wanted another daughter. I guess I got my wish after all."

Her words replayed in my mind for the rest of the day all the way until our wheels touched down in Chicago the next morning. When reality was no longer something to ignore.

My first day back at work was torture. I got way too used to working remotely for the two weeks we were at Graham's family's farm. Only checking my email on occasion, only pouring over case studies and files when it was late, and night had settled around us. We moved on different time than we do here in the city. Everything's relaxed and unhurried, unlike home, where everyone seems to be in a hurry to go nowhere at all.

After the day I've had, my feet ache so bad, I can feel it in my bones. Wearing stilettos and being almost six months pregnant with not one but two babies, do not go together, and I am quickly realizing that after how badly the arches of my feet hurt.

"Let me see," Graham says softly from the other end of my couch.

"No, I'll be fine. I just need to lie here for a minute."

Since we've been home, I've been trying to put *some* kind of distance between us but failing.

Terribly.

Our trip changed things between us, whether I was ready to admit it or not, and now I feel like the situation is out of my control.

I'm desperately clinging to being "friends." Whatever the hell that even means anymore.

Without asking again, he picks up my aching foot and places it in his lap, tenderly running his thumb down the sole of it, massaging my arch.

"Oooooh," I moan, sinking further into the couch as my eyes roll back. There are few things in the world that feel this good.

And most of them come from the man rubbing my foot *almost* as well as he does those other things.

His calloused fingers feel like heaven against my sensitive skin, and I hold back a shiver as he leans down and brushes his lips over my calf.

"Graham..." I warn.

Lifting his hands in defense, he grins smugly. "What? I'm just trying to make it feel better."

"I feel like I swallowed two bowling balls. And I look like I swallowed a whole planet."

"You're beautiful. Perfection," Graham says, his eyes never leaving mine.

"You only say that because I'm having your kids."

His fingers brush along the bottom of my foot, tickling me until I'm thrashing in his arms. He looks at me with a teasing grin, his eyebrows raised, as if saying try me.

"Fine, stop, stop," I plead.

"That's not true and you know it. You've always been the most beautiful girl in any room you were in, Emery, now... well, I can't take my eyes off you. No matter where we are, I find myself searching for you."

Lately, I don't know who I'm trying to convince more, Graham or myself, that these feelings don't exist.

That my heart doesn't do a traitorous little pitter patter when he says things like this.

"You're not so bad yourself, Adams." I sit up on my elbows, peering over my stomach. "I was thinking. Tomorrow, when we find out what the babies are... would you be okay with it just being us? I love the idea of having a gender reveal with family and friends, but I also don't. If that makes sense?"

"I'm good with whatever you wanna do, Em, always."

"It's just... I think it feels more special, if it's just us and the babies. The calm before the storm. My baby shower will be happening in the next month, not to mention Holland's and I just feel like this will be the last moment we have as just us before our families take over. I'm grateful that we have such an amazing support system, don't get me wrong."

He stops me. "No, I get it. Everyone's excited. First babies, and twins at that. Hell, I'm so excited I can't stand it sometimes, so I understand what they're feeling. What if we find out the gender together, later? After the appointment, when it's just the two of us."

Honestly? It sounds perfect, and exactly what I imagined.

"We can have the ultrasound technician write the gender down, and then we can drop it off at the bakery. They can fill a cupcake, so we can be surprised."

"Fuck, I'm excited, Em. It makes all of this much more real, you know?"

I nod, placing a hand on the flurry of movement in my stomach.

Graham's eyes dart down to my stomach.

"Can I talk to them?" he asks quietly, nodding at my stomach. "The babies?"

"Of course. They're really active tonight."

He rises and puts my feet back on the couch before sinking to his knees next to me. Tenderly, he places his hand on my stomach and rubs.

"Hey baby beans, it's your daddy."

Oh god, I'm going to cry. I wasn't emotionally prepared for how... *sweet* it would be to see Graham on his knees, talking to our babies. His brow is furrowed in concentration, like finding the right words is the most important thing he'll ever do.

His throat bobs as he swallows, then he leans forward and begins speaking to them, "I can't wait to find out what you're going to be tomorrow, but if my gut is right... you're girls. That's scary as fu-... I mean heck. I don't know much about girls, but I do know that even if I somehow mess everything up... well, I'll love you both more than you'll ever know."

A tear falls before I can stop it, and he looks up when I sniffle, then reaches out shakily and swipes the fallen tear away with his thumb. Delicately. Tenderly.

It makes my chest ache.

Still holding my gaze, he continues speaking to the babies, but it feels like he's speaking directly to me.

"I'll do everything I can to make you happy, and I'll never be the one to make you cry. I'll be the one to wipe away your tears and show you that it'll be okay. You and your mama are my whole life."

Oh god, my heart. It can't take this. The emotion in his face is palpable. I can feel it hanging around us both, the ferocity of his words and what he feels for our babies.

"I know that I'm probably going to make a bunch of mistakes before I get it right. I'll forget things and lose your bows all over the house. Burn dinner. Miss practices. I'm bound to forget your favorite dress-up outfit. But I'll always show up. I'll always be there when you need me. Your biggest fan on the sidelines, and I know that you'll both be mine. When I'm on the ice, I can't wait to look over and see you there with your mama cheering me on. I wanna be your best friend just like my dad was mine. I promise I'll love you, forever and a day. Always." He clears his throat, rubbing his hand tenderly back and forth over my round belly before leaning forward and placing a kiss there.

"Graham..." I whisper. Emotion settles in my throat, causing the words I want to say to be lost. They disappear before I can even utter them.

Even long after he's left, promising to be back bright and early for our appointment, I replay his words in my head.

And when I sleep, I dream of Graham.

"I'm nervous. But in a good way, the exciting way where I haven't been able to sit still all day. Or that could be the twelve bottles of water I drank so the babies would be active for the ultrasound," I say.

Graham squeezes my hand gently, and I smile. His excitement is infectious. His leg has been nervously bouncing since we got to my house after our appointment... then stopping at the bakery. We're sitting on the floor of what will be the babies' makeshift room, two cupcakes sitting in the box between us. They're nondescript. Plain white icing, with a white holder.

No hints, not one clue about what's inside.

This is it. The moment we've been waiting for.

Once we take a bite, we'll know what our babies are.

It's a big moment, and... I'm thankful that I have Graham here with us. I'm even more grateful he agreed to do it with just the two of us.

It makes the moment even more special to me. A bubble of just us. Before the world around us erupts in excited chaos.

He's convinced they're girls, but honestly, I'm not sure. Sometimes I think they're boys, and others, I'm convinced they're girls that'll look just like their daddy.

Either way... I'm happy. All I want is two healthy, happy babies and I'll be content.

I think back to when we found out I was pregnant and how badly Graham wanted boys, but now he has completely changed his tune.

I've seen Graham with Olive. How patient, attentive, and gentle he is with her. He's exactly the way his mother described him, hard exterior but soft and tender on the inside. Except when it comes to those he loves.

"Last guess, Davidson, what's your money on?" He grins, glancing down at the cupcakes between us.

"Hmmm. Boys."

He shakes his head. "Let's do this. The anticipation is fucking killing me."

I laugh and nod.

We each pick up a cupcake, and I start the countdown, "One... two... Three."

At the same time, we take a bite out of our cupcake. My eyes are glued to Graham's cupcake, well what's left of it, and the pink icing smeared along his lips.

"Graham," I screech around my mouthful of cupcake, "It's girls!"

"Fuck yes! I knew it."

Scrambling from the floor he jumps up and pulls me to him, crushing me to his body in a hug, spinning me around the room.

I'm barely holding on to what's left of the cupcake, giggling until I feel the tears wet my cheeks.

It's the most wholesome, pure moment I've ever experienced, and no matter what happens after this... I'll never forget this feeling.

"God, I'm so fucking happy, Em. Now we get to name them."

He sets me gently down back on my feet but doesn't let go. His arms stay circled around my back, rubbing gently along the strip of skin peeking out from my top. I inhale his scent, trying not to lean farther into his touch.

"Girls. I'd be the luckiest guy in the world if they look just like you, Davidson." He brushes his thumb along my lip, and I nip at him, grazing my teeth along the tip of his finger playfully.

I feel his laugh in my stomach, the butterflies erupting and dancing inside me.

"Dark hair, those gorgeous baby blues, feisty, confident. Independent."

I smirk. "They'll probably grow up with a hockey stick in their hand if you or Reed have anything to say about it."

"Well, they're growing up in a family of hockey players, babe. Comes with the territory. Plus, we're both competitive as hell, so I'm sure that's another trait they'll get."

I bring the rest of my cupcake to my lips and stick my tongue out, flicking the icing off the top. Graham's eyes darken as he watches.

I've learned in the past few weeks just how much I like Graham watching me. Doing lots of things.

"Keep licking that cupcake like that Emery Davidson, and we'll make a mess."

I raise my eyebrows. "Is that so?"

Another flick of my tongue. The vanilla icing melts in my mouth. One second, I'm devouring the cupcake, and the next, Graham's picking me up, bridal style, and carrying me to the bedroom.

Somehow, before the night is over, I'm covered in icing, but I'm not complaining, not one bit.

GRAHAM

NINETEEN

I FUCKING *LOVE* PREGNANCY.

Listen, I know I don't have to go through the process of birth, or the actual carrying of the babies for nine months but seeing Emery pregnant is the best thing in my life.

Hands down, no question.

I'm so damn crazy about her, I can't keep my hands off of her, which works out since she's horny as fuck. When I say horny, I mean like I'm putting together cribs one second, the next, she's on top of me, riding me like her life depends on it.

She can't get enough, and I'm happy to oblige. I love everything about her body, even more now while she's carrying my babies.

We spent the majority of the day putting stuff on the registry for the girls, and now that we're back home at Emery's, she's been eye-fucking me across the couch for the last ten minutes.

Which I've been ignoring.

Why?

Because I'm not caving and giving her the D until she admits that she likes me. Juvenile? Maybe.

But, it's all part of my plan to make her fall in love with me.

I just have to get her to be honest with herself, and with me. Even though I know the truth.

It's been an entire day since I've been inside her, and the longer she looks at me with those eyes, I feel myself wavering.

Slightly.

I'm also not one to back down, so...

Twenty minutes into this movie and I have no idea what in the fuck is happening, but my eyes stay glued to the television, until I feel her toes slide up my calf then back down. Soft and sensual, trying to get my attention.

It fucking works.

I look over at her, and she's looking up at me through her dark lashes, her lip between her teeth, knowing exactly what she's doing.

Fuck. Fuck.

It takes everything inside me, but I manage to look away and pretend to focus on the tv. Why in the hell does she have to be the hottest woman on the planet? And why the hell can't she just actually be mine?

I want to groan. My dick is hard, pressing against my gym shorts.

Seconds later, I hear a "hmph," and I smirk.

Yeah babe, I know exactly what you're doing, and it won't work.

I feel her get up from the couch and walk to her bedroom. Then her door slams, and a few minutes of silence pass.

Wait.

She didn't go in there to use....

My ass is off the couch before I can even blink, sprinting

toward her bedroom. When I throw the door open, the very last thing I expect to see is Emery wearing nothing but the sexiest piece of clothing I've ever seen in my life.

My fucking jersey, and absolutely nothing else.

I bring my fist to my mouth and hold back the groan that's about to explode from my chest.

God damnit. Game over. She fucking won.

"Adams," she grins smugly, "you don't mind if I wear this do you?"

"Nmph." I groan in response. I can't find words; I'm fucking speechless. Emery wearing my jersey is forever burned into my brain.

Perfection. Plain and fucking simple.

My dick is threatening to punch through the fabric of my shorts at any second, and I'm hanging by the thinnest thread possible.

"You know two can play at this game."

Rising on her knees, she crawls toward the end of the bed where I'm standing, reaching out and tracing her finger down my chest. "You know how much I like to win."

God, I'm fucking obsessed with my baby mama.

Nah, obsessed doesn't even *touch* it.

"Admit it. All you've gotta do is admit that you like me, and you feel something, Em." I bring my hand to her back, running my fingers along my name, then drag my hand lower and lower until I cup her ass in my hands.

She sucks in a breath.

Two *can* play this game, but I *always* play to win.

And it seems like my baby mama has been keeping score for a long time.

Gently, I lie her back on the bed, my hands sliding underneath the jersey to run down the soft skin of her sides.

"Graham."

My name falls breathlessly from her lips, and I smirk. I pull the jersey up slowly, exposing her stomach. Lately, she's been frustrated with herself for the weight she's gained and the marks along her lower stomach and sides.

I hate that she feels that way. That she's insecure about it. She's perfection, and I try to tell her every chance that I get.

I bring my lips to her stomach and plant kisses along the curve, till I make it to the scoring of pink marks along the front: jagged and angry, making them stand out against her skin.

They're fucking beautiful, and right now, just like this... She's never been sexier.

Never have I wanted her more.

And I hope she knows it as I kiss along the marks, taking my time with each one, looking up at her over the stretch of her belly.

"Need you to know something, Em. Not sure if you're ready to hear it, but I'm going to say it anyway."

My lips travel along the expanse of her stomach, making sure to kiss each and every one of the stretch marks.

"There's nothing that comes close to the sight of you, round and glowing with my babies in your belly. It drives me insane. At this rate, you'll be pregnant for the next ten years, and I plan to spend every minute of it worshiping you."

Her eyes go wide.

"I mean what I say, and even though you're not ready to admit to me or to yourself of what's actually happening between us, doesn't mean I'm going to dance around the truth."

Sliding my tongue lower, I settle between her legs, pushing her thighs farther apart so I can see her.

I feel how wound up she is, tight like a line, ready to pop at any moment, and I can't fucking wait to watch her fall apart. I skim my fingers lightly along her pussy, using my fingers to spread her open.

I could spend every waking moment, of every damn day, buried right between these thighs and die a happy man.

"Are you aching yet, baby?" I ask when I hear her inhale sharply, her hands fisting in the sheets as my tongue grazes her clit. "All day, you've been horny and restless, and I wouldn't give in. I bet you want to come so badly, don't you, Em?"

I'm relentlessly teasing her, barely touching her pussy. Only a graze, a simple brush of my fingers, a gentle touch of my tongue.

Enough to drive her wild.

I want to see her quivering beneath me, begging to be touched. And if she's a good girl, I'll give her what she wants.

"I bet you want me to suck your little clit in my mouth and bury my fingers inside of you. Is that what you want?"

Silence meets my question, so I pull back and crawl over her body, hovering there.

Her chest is rising and falling in pants, her eyes burning with want.

I use the same thumb that was just on her clit, to brush along the bottom of her lip as my eyes hold hers, spreading the taste of her on her lips.

"Do you want to come, baby? Do you want me to make it better?" I whisper, pulling the jersey up to display her tits.

My most favorite thing about pregnancy is how sensitive her tits are. One right move, and I set her off like fucking fireworks.

It's so goddamn sexy.

Her nipples have darkened to a dusty rose, and her tits are heavier. Preparing for motherhood. So supple and sweet, I want to take a bite.

I do, scraping my teeth along the pebbled flesh. I tug one nipple into my mouth, rolling it between my teeth and daring to let them graze the sensitive peak while I tweak the other with my free hand.

"Graham," she pants, threading her fingers in my hair as she moans. I grunt against her skin, giving special attention to each nipple, savoring the taste of her. "More, please."

Hearing Emery Davidson beg is better than I ever imagined it would be.

"Only because you asked so nicely." I smirk, tweaking her nipple one last time before I trail my way down her stomach, planting kisses as I go lower, settling between her legs once more.

The second my fingers connect with her clit, her back arches off the bed, a tremor running through her. I can feel her shake, just from my touch.

It makes me feral. Fucking wild.

I can't wait another second to taste her. Bringing my tongue to her pussy, I take a lazy, slow swipe. I spread her wider and slide my tongue from her clit to her opening, taking my time, driving her over the edge.

"Oh god..." She fists my hair, tugging hard. God damnit, I love when she shuts her head off and lets her body take over.

Seconds later, with my fingers deep inside her, she detonates, like the most delicious bomb in history. I lap at her pussy until she's sated and nothing but a pile of bones.

Emery looks up at me through heavy-lidded eyes, now languid and sleepy she grins.

"I'm not done with you yet, beautiful, I'm just getting started." I grin, moving up her body and nudging her legs open.

"All talk and no action, big guy."

I spend the rest of the afternoon showing her why I'm always going to be number one on that stupid scorecard of hers.

———

"Em, have you seen my phone?" I say, rounding the corner into the living room.

Except when I walk around the corner, Reed and Holland are standing by the front door with a giggling Emery.

"Adams, what the fuck!" Reed barks, reaching out to cover Holland's eyes with his hands.

Fuuuuck, after the mind-blowing sex I just had, and the fact that I had no idea her fucking brother was here, I'm butt-ass naked. I scramble to grab the closest thing to me to cover my junk, which just so happens to be a replica stuffed animal of Dr. Dickey that my sister sent to Emery's house as a joke.

God damnit.

"I'm sorry, fuck, I didn't know you were here!" I cry, trying to cover my balls and my dick with this tiny ass stuffed animal.

Emery's covering her mouth, trying to hold back the laughter, while Holland's trying to look around Reed's hands, feeling around like she's a blind person.

"What's happening?" Holland asks.

"Nothing that you need to see," Reed grumbles.

"Well, Graham is here, and I didn't expect either of you, so he's naked."

Holland squeaks, "Oh *shit*."

Reed turns a new shade of red, and I get ready to duck at any second because I'm sure as fuck, something is about to come flying at my head.

"Clothes! Now Adams!" he yells.

"Fuck, alright," I mutter, turning around and running back

to Em's room. I hear Emery making a comment to Holland about "butt dimples" before I slam the door behind me.

Great, just fantastic. It's bad enough that I knocked up my best friend's sister, now he has to witness my dick swinging in the wind at her house.

I quickly throw on my shorts and tee then walk back out to the living room. Emery loops her arm in Holland's and drags her toward the bedroom I just came out of.

"Trust me, we do not want to stay for this conversation."

And then the two of them are gone, leaving me with a pissed-off Reed.

Listen, the guy might be my best friend, but he hasn't forgiven me for sleeping with Emery, and he sure as shit hasn't forgiven me for getting her pregnant. Not to mention, you really don't want to be on his bad side.

I sit on the opposite end of the couch, keeping my distance.

Silence hangs between us for what feels like minutes before he speaks.

"I'm going to beat the shit out of you," he says so matter-of-factly.

"Figured. I deserve it, I guess. For sleeping with your sister."

He looks over at me, the same shade of blue in his eyes as Emery. "You fuck. It's not because you decided to sleep with my sister, it's because I know you and I know how you are. And I know that you'll hurt her."

"I'll never hurt her. Ever," I say assuredly. "I'm fucking crazy about her, Reed."

The look on his face shows he doesn't believe me, and hell, I don't blame him. I had fun; I didn't let shit hold me back. I had nothing to tie me down.

"Listen, I love her, Reed. I haven't told her that because

she'd probably block me and never speak to me again, but I fucking love her, and there's nothing I wouldn't do for her or my girls. Nothing. If you wanna kick my ass, fine. But I'm still going to love her, and I'm not going anywhere. You need to know that."

For a second, I think he might hit me, but he shakes his head. "If you hurt her, if you do anything to make her cry..." he trails off.

He doesn't even need to say it.

"We're on the same page."

He nods, not looking entirely convinced. "Still want to put my fist through your face."

"Noted."

"Uh," Holland calls from the doorway, "sorry to interrupt your heart-to-heart, but uh... we've got a problem."

Reed and I look at each other then back at Holland.

"What?" we say in unison.

"Grahaaaaaaam!!!" Emery screeches, pushing past Holland through the doorway of the kitchen. "Get the bag. Get the bag. Shit, get the bag!"

Wait, what?

"Emery's in labor." Holland screeches.

Reed and I look at each other again, momentarily frozen. Mostly in shock. That was not what either of us were expecting Holland to say.

"Graham!" Emery yells.

I scramble from the couch, realization hitting me.

Oh. Fuck.

The bag. That bag, the one that I packed with Emery six weeks ago just in case. That bag. THE bag.

Fuck. Shit, where are my car keys?

I'm rushing around her house like a fucking chicken with

my head cut off because apparently hearing the words "Emery's in labor" sends my brain over the edge.

"Graham."

"Okay, I'm grabbing the bags. The car seats are already installed in my truck, and I'll grab the stroller too just in case we need it. Reed, have you seen my keys? I swear I left them over th-"

"Graham."

Oh yeah, I forgot, I put them in the bathroom.

"Adams," Reed barks, halting me mid-step.

I glance over at Emery who's breathing heavily through her nose while Holland rubs her back gently.

"Shit, I'm sorry Em."

She smiles through a grimace, "It's okay. The bag?"

"Right, the bag. One second." I sprint to the girls room, grab the bag, and am back in the living room in fifteen seconds flat.

"I'm going to pull the car around, be right back." Reed says over his shoulder, disappearing out the front door, leaving me with Em and Holland.

I walk over, and lace my hand in hers, helping her towards the front door. Her face is scrunched in pain, and her hands remain on her stomach.

"Everything's going to be okay, babe. You've got this, and I'll be by your side the entire time."

Her eyes hold mine, and then suddenly her hand tightens around mine as another contraction hits her.

"Get me to the hospital... now. Before I have these babies on the floor."

GRAHAM

TWENTY

"THAT'S IT, baby, you're doing amazing. God, you're so fucking strong, and I'm so proud of you. So damn proud," I say as we go into another hard push, and the first cry fills the room around us.

That's our girl. God, I'm hearing my girls cry for the first time.

The most beautiful sound in the world.

She wails so loud it pierces the air, and I can't help but laugh as the tears fall down my face.

That's my baby.

My eyes glance back down at my beautiful girl, exhausted and worn out, but strong as ever.

I've never felt more pride, never been prouder of anyone or anything in my life as I am right now.

All I have to say is that after witnessing Emery giving birth to our babies, I have a newfound respect for women.

She is the strongest woman I've *ever* fucking seen, and I couldn't admire her any more than I do right now. Watching her push through the pain... It is the most humbling experience I've ever had.

I've broken bones, gotten into some bloody fights, had more stitches than I can even count, and I know nothing comes close to the pain she's experiencing right now.

And so gracefully, all for our girls.

I know without a shadow of a doubt, I'm in love with Emery Davidson. More now than ever.

I'll never forget this moment. Not as long as I live. She's resilient in ways that I could never be. Hell, if the tables were turned, I'd be crying like a baby; yet she grits her teeth and grips my hand harder, then pushes with all of her strength.

Another cry, and now both of our babies are screaming at the top of their lungs, arriving into the world in true Adams' fashion.

Reaching out, I push the sweat-drenched hair back from her forehead and plant my lips there as the nurse brings both girls and places them against Em's bare chest. They immediately quiet, nestling into her.

It makes me cry like a fucking baby.

My girls.

I've waited my entire life for this, and I had no idea. I had no idea that this moment would truly change everything.

I know now, there will be before this moment, and after. That's it.

Tears wet my cheeks as I peer down at them. So peaceful, so perfect, that my chest feels tight.

"Em, you did it, baby, look you did it. They're so beautiful. God, they're ours."

Em sobs, messy fat tears, that smear the makeup down her face, but god, she's so incredible.

"Congratulations Mom and Dad, two beautiful, healthy

baby girls. Now the real adventure starts," her doctor says, standing over my new family with a smile.

I lean down over the bed and run my finger down their noses. Button-like, and pink, they're so perfect that I can't even believe they are ours.

"They have your nose." She sobs so hard her shoulders are shaking.

"No, baby, they look just like you. *Perfect*," I say.

We have a few uninterrupted minutes before the nurse takes both girls and cleans them up, while another nurse attends to Em.

I don't want to be apart from the girls or Em, but I give Em privacy as the nurse helps her change into a new gown and get cleaned up. I watch as the nurse bathes the girls and weighs and measures them both.

"Baby A is seven pounds even, and Baby B is six pounds, seven ounces. We're going to bring them down to the NICU to test their breathing, and run a few more tests, but as soon as they are done, we'll bring them right back up," the nurse tells Em and me.

"I hate this part," Em whispers, watching as the girls are rolled out in clear bassinets. "I heard this would happen, but it sucks."

I kiss her head and stroke her arm. "I know, but they'll be back soon with a clean bill of health, and we won't have to be apart from them again."

She nods, tears in her deep blue eyes.

"I was thinking… for their names. I know we talked about a couple different names, but what about Charlotte Reed Adams, and Quinn Allie Adams?" she asks.

Fuck, naming the girls after Reed and Allie? Nothing in the world would make me happier. We both have such close relationships with our siblings, it makes perfect sense that our girls have a piece of them too."

"That's perfect, Em."

She nods, a small smile tugging at her lips. "I think so too. I think it fits them."

"Me too."

Her eyes hold mine for a moment, and she opens her mouth to speak but then closes it.

It feels like there's so much to say, and so much I want to say, but I want to hold on to this moment.

An hour later, the nurse wheels Charlotte and Quinn back into the room, then places them in my arms. The nurse leaves a few things for Em then exits, leaving us all alone for the very first time. I'm sitting right next to Emery, who's dozed off from pure exhaustion. She tried to keep her eyes open as long as she could, but her body needed rest. She just did the most incredible thing in the world, birthing our babies, and she needs to replenish her energy.

Plus, it gives me a second with the girls before they become Mama's girls.

With Charlotte on my left, and Quinn on my right, I watch them as their little lips pucker in sleep, dreams dancing behind their eyes. Well, at least I think that babies dream.

"I feel like I've waited so long for this moment, but now that you're here, it feels like I don't have long enough with you. Before I've got to share you with everyone else. That sounds selfish, I know. I just... I don't want to share you just yet. Only with your mama."

When I look up, I see Em's eyes open, staring directly at me, filled with tears.

I grin. "I can't believe we get to be parents to these beautiful girls." I lean down again, pretending to whisper to them, "I know you probably don't know this yet, but you've got the most beautiful mama in the world, and you look just like her. Except, I think you're even prettier."

Emery laughs. "Always the Casanova, Adams."

Shrugging, I stand carefully and walk the girls over to Em, gently setting them in her arms.

She stares at them both, love and adoration in her eyes, and I'm so proud in this moment to be their dad.

To be her partner, in whatever sense.

One thing I know, without a doubt and with upmost certainty, I'm in love with Emery Davidson, and I won't stop until she's mine and our family is together, just the way it should be.

EMERY

TWENTY-ONE

CHARLOTTE AND QUINN ADAMS are the pieces of my heart that I was missing all along. Truthfully, I never knew that I was incomplete until I held them in my arms for the first time. Touched their button noses, their tiny little lips. Watched their eyelids flutter, and their chests rise and fall with each breath.

Now, I can't imagine ever living life without them. Even now, my life *before* them seems like a distant memory. Nothing compares to the feeling that I feel now.

It's early, maybe around seven a.m., and I've just fed them both and gotten them back to sleep. Thankfully, breastfeeding has been easy so far, which I know isn't usually the case, and especially not with twins, so I'm thankful. But Graham and I both stayed up most of the night just staring at them, talking, and enjoying the time together.

Graham passed out sometime around three a.m., but the second the girls started to cry, his eyes popped open and he flew out his chair so fast he tripped over his shoe and face planted on the floor.

It was so adorable and hilarious that I cried laughing so hard.

My sweet girls are still sleeping soundly in my arms, while their daddy snores softly beside us. He's slumped back in the recliner, one hand still resting on my bed. He's worried he'll miss something, or not wake when the girls do.

The tv plays in the background. Something about sports that Graham put on to have background noise. Just him and me with our girls.

It's the first time in a long time I've felt this much peace and happiness, all in one.

Content.

I watch the girls sleep, unable to take my eyes off them. It's all I've been able to do since the nurse brought them back to us. I'm scared if I blink, I'll miss something.

There were a lot of things I learned today. Not just becoming a mother for the first time, or how to get the babies to latch on to nurse.

I realized that I'm falling in love with Graham Adams, and that terrifies me.

It's not that I didn't think about it prior to this moment, it's just seeing him with his girls. How tender and gentle and how much love he has for them. It's in the way that he cared for me, encouraged me, supported me, pushed me when I felt like giving up.

He's selfless, caring, and protective. Kind and thoughtful.

He's everything I want in a man, and that scares me. Giving my heart to anyone after being hurt, after deciding I didn't want the white-picket life.

Graham took everything I thought I wanted and showed me it was nothing that I thought it would be.

I've spent the last nine months falling, little by little.

Piece by piece. Inch by inch, he worked his way into my heart, and now... I don't know what my future looks like without him.

Without us as a family.

"You okay, babe?"

I look up and Graham's sitting up in the recliner, sleep still heavy in his eyes as he yawns.

"I'm good. I was just trying to hold on to this moment, you know? I'm scared I'll blink, and it'll pass us by."

He nods. "That's how I feel too, but you also need rest, Em. You did something incredible today, and your body needs rest. Want me to hold them for a bit?"

I nod.

He stands, then walks over and takes the girls from me, taking his spot back on the couch. I watch as he smiles and talks to them in what I like to call his "Hot dad" voice.

I mean honestly, men with their babies are a whole different breed.

And watching him with the girls makes my heart swell so impossibly much, it feels like I can't... I can't fall any further for him, but then he does something that causes me to.

"Reed and everyone are going to be here in the next few hours. I talked to him a little while ago. He said Mom is coming with new outfits for the girls, and Holland won't stop talking about how she's an aunt. She's due any minute now."

Graham nods. "I can't wait for the guys to meet them. They're going to have the best uncles in the world."

I nod, agreeing, knowing that my brother and their friends will be amazing with the girls, just like they are with Evan and Olive.

"I can't believe they're finally here, Em," Graham says, still rocking the girls on his chest.

"Breaking news," the sportscaster says on the tv screen, causing me to look over.

Graham and I both look up as the camera cuts to a new screen in a newsroom. The male anchor sits next to the morning tv host.

"Guys, we've just gotten word that there is breaking news. Our source says you're hearing it here first, so we're bringing this to you live from our newsroom. It looks like Graham Adams has been traded from the Chicago Avalanches to the Washington Warriors. Adams' time in Chicago has officially come to an end."

TO BE CONTINUED....

Pickup the highly anticipated conclusion of Graham and Emery's story here.

THE FINAL SCORE

INTERNATIONAL BESTSELLING AUTHOR
MAREN MOORE

WHAT'S NEXT?

THE EX EQUATION

MAREN MOORE

A brand new enemies with benefits standalone featuring a brand new world!

WHAT'S NEXT?

Grumpy sunshine
Second chance
Small town
Fake dating

Preorder your copy HERE!

ABOUT THE AUTHOR

Be the first to know!
Sign up for all updates here:
https://geni.us/NLMaren

Top 20 Amazon Bestselling author, Maren Moore writes romantic sports comedies with alpha daddies. Her heroines are best friend material, and you can always expect a HEA with lots of spice. When she isn't in front of her computer writing you can find her curled up with her kindle, binge watching Netflix, or chasing after her little ones.

Printed in Great Britain
by Amazon